DANNY ORLIS
AND THE
MYSTERY OF THE SUNKEN SHIP

DANNY ORLIS
AND THE
MYSTERY OF THE SUNKEN SHIP

BERNARD PALMER

Please note that several books in the Danny Orlis series are published by Sword of the Lord Publications and are available for purchase on their website, www.swordbooks.com.

Aneko Press *Youth*

www.anekopress.com

Aneko Press, Life Sentence Publishing, and our logos are trademarks of Life Sentence Publishing, Inc.
203 E. Birch Street
P.O. Box 652
Abbotsford, WI 54405

JUVENILE FICTION / Religious / Christian / Action & Adventure
Paperback ISBN: 978-1-62245-992-6
eBook ISBN: 978-1-62245-993-3
10   9   8   7   6   5   4   3   2   1
Available where books are sold

CONTENTS

CHAPTER 1

QUIPS ON THE DOCK

It was late afternoon in coastal Guatemala where Danny and Kay Orlis were serving as missionaries. Palm trees swayed and their fronds rustled in the brisk wind whipping down from the highlands and across the jungle since morning. But the wind brought no relief to the steaming forest.

The sun on the rim of the horizon was ready to slip away for a night of rest, without one last gesture of defiance. Its blazing rays still fueled the fiery wind. The heat seemed to have continued to build through the day. A stifling, suffocating heat snatched breath from laboring lungs and soaked clothing with perspiration at the slightest exertion.

Life at the Mission had seemed suspended during the middle of the day and only now was it beginning to stir. Danny Orlis, who had been lying down for half an hour or so, arose wearily and wiped the perspiration that beaded his forehead.

"I thought the wind might cut the heat a little," he said to Kay, "but it's as bad now as it's been."

Kay Orlis went to the refrigerator and poured a glass of water. Her youthful face was pinched and thin; dark shadows lurked beneath her eyes.

"I know," she said, her voice weary and weak. "I wonder what it would be like to be where it's cool enough to sleep the whole night through."

Danny went to the door of their little house and looked out toward the harbor. For several minutes he stared at the blue-green waters of the Gulf. There was a speck on the horizon, a tiny, bobbing speck. At first, he could determine no movement, but after a time it seemed to be headed toward the Mission.

"Where are the binoculars, Kay?"

"I'll get them," Kay replied.

She handed him the field glasses he had brought from Northwest Angle, Minnesota, and he focused them carefully.

"She's coming this way, all right," he said.

"What kind of a boat is it?" Kay Orlis asked.

Danny shook his head. "It's still too far away to tell," he said. "I think she must be a fishing boat of some sort. She's not very big, but she's a sturdy, seaworthy little craft. Reminds me of the kind of boats that run on the Lake of the Woods."

Danny went into the other room and got his hat.

"Where are you going, Danny?"

He grinned self-consciously. "I thought I'd wander down to the dock," he said. "I guess I haven't changed much since I was a kid. Whenever a boat came in at the Angle, I was there."

"Wait a minute," his young wife said. "I'll go along."

They left the house and walked down the narrow, palm-lined path to the harbor. Once or twice Danny stopped and peered through the binoculars.

"I can't make out the name," he said. "But I've seen that boat somewhere."

"I can't understand why anyone would want to put in here," Kay observed as they passed the last row of houses and approached the sagging dock. "The village doesn't have much in the way of supplies to sell; the harbor here doesn't afford any real protection in case of a storm."

Danny laughed.

"Now don't try to make such a mystery of it, Kay. There's undoubtedly a very good reason for the boat to put in. They may need supplies, or it could be someone wants to look over the Mission."

"It could be," Kay answered doubtfully. "Usually visitors contact us first."

Danny and Kay were almost at the dock when there was a yell, then the sound of scurrying feet behind them.

"Danny!" a youthful voice called. "Danny! Wait up! Wait for us!"

"Mark and Matt Maxwell!" Danny exclaimed. They both stopped and turned to face the boys. "Where do you think you're going?"

"The same place you are," Matt said looking impish. "Down to see the boat come in."

The two boys were about twelve years old and about the same size. In fact they looked so much alike that their mother (she claimed to be able to tell them apart) had grabbed the wrong one more than once and spanked him for something his twin brother had done.

"You guys had better be careful," Danny said. "You get down here and pull some of your shenanigans and the guys on that boat will dump you both into the harbor."

"We're not scared," Mark said boastfully.

Matt walked beside Kay.

"Know something, Kay?" he said, his eyes beginning to shine. "That's a pirate ship. When they get into the dock they'll probably hoist the Jolly Roger and kidnap us all for ransom."

"If they kidnapped you," Kay answered, "it wouldn't be long until they'd bring you back."

"We wouldn't take him back, would we, Kay?" Mark cut in.

The four were not the only ones who had seen the boat making its way toward shore and had come down to the dock to investigate. Mr. Hale, the genial Mission superintendent, was already there with his wife. He was a tall man, thin as a coconut palm, and as bald as a conch shell. Years in the tropics had turned his skin to a crinkled, leathery brown.

"Hello, Mr. and Mrs. Hale," the twins said respectfully.

"Good afternoon, boys," Mel Hale answered. "I thought you were still confined to quarters."

The color rose to their cheeks.

"Aw," Mark said, "that was yesterday."

"I never did get the straight of it," Mel continued. "Just what did you do that caused the trouble?"

"Well," Mark began, "we've got company from the States. Miss Selma Anderson who used to go to school with Mom."

"She's scared of snakes and bugs and everything," the other boy added contemptuously. "She won't leave the house or anything."

"What did you do?" Kay asked seriously.

"Nothin' much," Mark replied. "We just put a couple of bull frogs in the bed. That's all."

Danny had to turn away.

"It really wasn't very nice to do a thing like that, was it?" Kay asked.

"We went this morning," Matt said, "and apologized. We asked her to forgive us."

"You did the right thing," Mr. Hale approved.

While they had been talking, the boat was plowing steadily toward them.

"Recognize her, Mel?" Danny asked after a time.

The superintendent nodded.

"I didn't at first," Mel said, "but she's beginning to look familiar. I think she is the *JUANITA MIA*, Captain Miguel D'Armando's boat."

Danny's forehead grew creases.

"Don't you remember him?" Melvin Hale continued. "He put in here about a year ago during a storm. He and his crew were weathered in for about a week."

"I remember," Danny said. "He's the one you led to Christ."

The superintendent nodded.

"I've never seen anyone as concerned about the things of Christ as Miguel after he became a Christian," he said. "I only wish he could have stayed for a few more weeks so I could have continued to teach him the Bible. He was so eager to learn."

The *JUANITA MIA* was an old boat, considerably larger than Danny had supposed she would be. Bigger and older.

That the boat was well cared for he could tell at a glance. The paint was new, and her deck was clean. The strong odors of less lovingly cared-for boats were conspicuously absent.

Apparently painted with regularity, the paint on the hull of the boat was so thick it was beginning to chip and peel away. She was caked with scale and her ornate superstructure spoke eloquently of age. For all that, she was trim of line and as sturdy looking as the Matterhorn. This was a strong-beamed, rough-water boat, one that could shake off the green breakers defiantly.

The craft was under charter. Danny could see the passengers lining the rail. They waved as the cumbersome *JUANITA MIA* was being warped.

"Look!" Mark exclaimed, nudging his twin. "There's a guy our age!"

They looked at one another.

"Do you suppose he's a greenhorn?" Matt asked.

"If they stay around a little while," Mark muttered, "we'll find out."

"Now boys," Kay warned, "remember . . . guest."

"Sure, Kay," Matt grinned. "We'll remember."

"We'll think about it while we're giving him a hard time," Mark added.

They turned their attention to the boy on deck.

"Come to think of it," Matt said appraisingly, "he looks a little bigger than we are. Maybe we'd better be kind after all."

"I know," Mark put in. "Pretend this is 'Be Kind to Dumb Greenhorns Week.' Then we won't spoil our record."

"Good idea," Matt responded. "I don't feel much like initiating a tenderfoot."

"You guys!" Danny reached out and rumpled Matt's hair. "If anyone who didn't know you listened, they'd think you were fugitives from juvenile hall."

"We wouldn't be *very* hard on him," Mark said. "We'd just give him a hard time the way we did to you and Kay when you came down here."

"You know," Matt said. "Good, clean fun."

Danny laughed.

"I don't think I'll ever forget," he said.

The boat was big for the little dock; she had to creep alongside. The engines were turning slowly, and the voices of the people on deck drifted to the knot of waiting missionaries.

"How long are we going to be here, Captain?" a tall, square-shouldered American demanded irritably. His voice was loud and arrogant.

He was new to the tropics; Danny could tell at first glance. His face and neck, fiery red, had blistered and were starting to peel. His cheeks shone with medication.

"How long are we going to be here?" he repeated, his voice rising. "When I speak, answer!"

Captain D'Armando shook his head and shrugged his shoulders expressively.

The sunburned one turned to a gray-haired man at his elbow.

"I don't see why you didn't get us a boat with an English-speaking captain, Adrian," he complained. "I haven't been able to make this man understand a thing since we left port."

"Quit griping, will you, Lars?" Adrian snapped. "That's all we've heard for the past week."

"A nice, congenial lot, aren't they, Kay?" Danny whispered.

"Maybe they're tired," she answered. "We shouldn't be too quick to judge."

Danny put his arm about her shoulder.

Captain D'Armando came to the rail and waved to the Mission superintendent.

"*Señor* Hale!" he exclaimed, beaming. "*Señor* Hale!"

Moments later he came bustling ashore to take Melvin Hale's hand eagerly.

"It's good to see you, Miguel," Mel said in Spanish.

"How many times I thank God for sending me to this place that time last year," the captain continued. "To think, it was a storm that caused me to put in here where you could show me the way to salvation."

"God works in strange ways," Mr. Hale reminded him.

"When I saw we come so close by you," Miguel said, "I could not help but stop!"

CHAPTER 2

BOAT PASSENGERS COME TO DINNER

The passengers had either left the JUANITA MIA and had come onto the dock or were standing on the deck, looking about curiously.

"Let's go over and introduce ourselves, Kay," Danny said, taking her by the arm.

Mark and Matthew Maxwell trotted with them.

"My name's Orlis," Danny said, holding out his hand.

"I'm Wilbur Adrian," the tall, gray-haired man said genially. Danny took him to be leader of the group.

"This is my wife, Kay," Danny continued.

Matt and Mark grinned at the boy standing beside Mr. Adrian.

"My name's Matt."

"And I'm Mark."

"We're twins," Matt then explained.

"Hi," the strange boy said. "I'm Gil Adrian."

This fellow was half a head taller than the Maxwell boys, broad shouldered, and heavily built, like a football player. Yet, he must have been about their age.

"Am I ever glad to see you guys," Gil said. "I was about to go goofy on board ship with nothing to do."

"How long are you going to be around?" Matt asked. "We'll take you fishin' and swimmin'."

Gil shrugged.

"Mr. Krotter was screaming about even stopping here," he said, "but it didn't do any good. Captain D'Armando stopped, and I'm sure glad he did. This is great!"

While the twins and Gil were talking, Mr. Adrian introduced Danny and Kay to others in the party.

"This is Lars Krotter," he said, indicating the sunburned fellow. "He'd rather fish than eat."

"That's what we ought to be doing right now," Lars grumbled.

"And this is Prescott," Mr. Adrian went on, ignoring Krotter's complaint.

A smiling, dark-haired girl of sixteen or so came up. Mr. Adrian turned.

"And here is my daughter, Dixie," he said. "The men still on board are Stan Wheeler and Brad Simmons. Stan is Prescott's nephew, and Simmons is a fellow we met in Belize. We're a bunch of amateurs out here, you see. He's going to teach us to dive."

Danny Orlis glanced up to see Simmons staring at him coldly from the deck of the ship. The stranger was not a big man, but shoulders and chest were heavily muscled, and his small gray eyes had a strange, bold fire.

Simmons knew they were talking about him, Danny realized. And moreover, the guy didn't like it.

As soon as Melvin Hale could leave Captain D'Armando, he went to Mr. Adrian, introduced himself, and met other members of the party.

"We'd like to have you all be guests for dinner this evening," he said.

"Oh, that would be wonderful!" Dixie squealed with excitement. "The cook on the *JUANITA MIA* seems to specialize in hot Spanish dishes. I've eaten about all of them that I can."

Mr. Adrian and Danny went aboard to invite the two on deck.

"Sure thing," Stan Wheeler said. He was about Dixie's age, perhaps a little older. "I'll be ready as soon as I change clothes."

Brad Simmons refused.

"To put it blunt-like, Gov'nor," he said, addressing Danny, "I ain't fixin' to put myself in a place where no preacher can get to hammerin' at me."

He was staring with almost open hostility at Danny.

"I'm sure Mr. Hale only wanted to be kind," Mr. Adrian said reproachfully.

"I'm goin' to let you in on something," Brad Simmons continued. He had been leaning against a bulkhead when they came on deck and had not moved. "You never saw a preacher do nothin' for nobody 'less he had a good reason for it and was goin' to get somethin' out of it. I'll go along with you most any place, Adrian, but here is one place where you can include me out."

"You'll be the only one aboard," Mr. Adrian reminded him. "I'm not sure, but I think the cook will not be preparing anything."

Brad Simmons spat contemptuously on the deck.

"Let me tell you, I'd starve first!" Simmons lashed out bitterly.

Danny and Mr. Adrian left the boat.

"Sometimes I wonder," the tall man said pensively, "whether we made a mistake in letting Brad Simmons come along."

* * *

Danny and Kay Orlis and the Maxwell family were invited to the Hale home for dinner. The two Orlises hurried back to their little cottage, showered, and changed clothes quickly.

"I want to go over and help Wilma as soon as I can," Kay said. "Honestly, Danny, I don't know how she can have so many people come in like this at the last minute. If it happened to me, I–I–I don't know what I would do."

"Maybe I'd better begin to follow Mel's example," he said. "I could invite a few people in for dinner at the last minute every now and then – just get you used to the idea."

A horrified look crossed Kay's face.

"Danny!" she exclaimed. "You wouldn't, would you? You wouldn't do a thing like that!"

Danny laughed.

As they walked to the Hale home, he turned to her.

"You've met Adrian and the others," he said. "What do you think of them?"

"They seem nice enough," Kay answered. "Why? What makes you ask?"

Danny was silent.

"I suppose they are all right," he said finally, "but I can't help thinking about Brad Simmons. I can't help it, Kay. I just don't trust that man."

"He did look coarse," Kay said.

"I told you of his reference to ministers and missionaries," Danny went on. "I suppose that could be why I distrust him. I don't believe that's entirely it, though. To me he seems to be so—so evil."

Kay's lips compressed.

"He seems different from the others," she observed. "Why do you suppose they would take up with him, include him on a cruise? I heard Mr. Adrian say they only met him in Belize. They couldn't have known him too long."

"That's something I can't figure out," Danny answered. "To tell you the truth, it bothers me."

When they reached the Hale home, Kay went directly to the kitchen to help Wilma while Danny Orlis joined the Mission superintendent and Captain D'Armando in the living room.

"I'm so glad you could come over this evening, Danny," Mel said in Spanish so his guest, the captain, could understand. "Miguel would like to spend an hour or so studying the Scriptures with me. We thought probably you could entertain the other guests meanwhile."

"Certainly," Danny Orlis replied. "I'd be glad to do that."

"That is good," Miguel D'Armando said. "There are so many things I do not yet understand about the Bible. So many things my heart aches for to know. When we go close by on this trip I say, 'We will stop here for the night.' They do not like it, but anyway, we stop."

Danny studied the boat captain. Miguel was swarthy and round-faced, with piercing dark eyes and a thin-line moustache on his upper lip. He was so weathered by the climate of the tropics that he could have been any age. Danny guessed him to be as old as Mel Hale or perhaps a little older.

Other guests came soon. And to Danny's surprise, Brad Simmons was among them. He had shaved two weeks' stubble from his face and was attired in clean clothes. He looked younger, but wrinkles still marked his face. Open insolence showed in his eyes.

Then Brad Simmons grinned.

"Evenin', Gov'nor," he addressed Danny. "S'prised to see me tonight, I take it."

"Frankly," Danny replied, answering look with look, "after what you said on the boat a little while ago, I am surprised. I thought you didn't want to come."

"You don't know me, Gov'nor," Simmons went on. "I always like to have my little joke. Fooled you, didn't I?"

"Let's say you convinced me," Danny countered. "At any rate I'm glad you did decide to come."

Simmons' smile disappeared.

"But mind you," he warned, "I want no preachin'. That's one thing I don't take too kindly. I am what I am, and I want nobody tryin' to change me."

Wilbur Adrian broke in just then.

"I told Brad *you* wouldn't insult him," he said pointedly.

"Of course not," Danny answered. "We preach the gospel and are always glad for an opportunity to talk with anyone about the Lord Jesus Christ. We know that no good can come from being insulting to people."

"See, Brad," Adrian said over his shoulder. "There's nothing to be afraid of."

Mrs. Hale and Kay entered the living room at this point.

"Would you like to come to the kitchen with Wilma and me?" Kay asked Dixie Adrian. "You can sit and visit while we take care of the dinner."

"Why don't you and Dixie sit here and visit, Kay?" Mrs. Hale suggested graciously. "The Maxwells are coming up the walk now. I'll get Doris to help."

Gil Adrian jumped to his feet.

"The Maxwells?" he echoed. "Are the kids with them?"

There was a sharp knock at the door and Gil hurried toward it. Matt and Mark came in.

"Hey, guys!" he said. "I didn't know you two were coming."

"We get around," Matt replied.

They went to a corner and sat down for a few minutes.

"Why don't we go outside?" Gil suggested. "Too many people in here."

"Okay," Mark said, "but we can't go so far away we won't hear Mrs. Hale call dinner. Wow, can she cook!"

"Do you suppose we could get Mrs. Hale to cook on the *JUANITA MIA*?" Gil asked.

* * *

Kay Orlis was studying Dixie as she talked with her. The girl was happy and light-hearted, with eyes that danced even when the smile was absent from her small, attractive face. She had an open, straight-for-ward look. She was a person one liked, instinctively, from the introduction.

"I suppose you've been having a good time on your trip," Kay said.

"Frankly," Dixie told her, "it's been something of a bore, so far."

The Orlis girl looked rather than voiced a question.

"I should think a cruise such as you're on would be delightful," she ventured. "Something you would always remember."

"Oh, yes," Dixie said, "but I'm actually more

interested in underwater photography than in fishing, and I haven't had a chance to do much diving."

"Oh," Kay echoed, "do you dive?"

"I love it!" the other girl exclaimed, her face lighting up. "That's the main reason I came with Dad. We both thought there would be plenty of time for me to dive. The men have insisted on fishing all the time, and I haven't had a chance to do anything I've wanted to do."

"The water around here is good for diving and underwater photography," Kay told her. "I've never done any of it, but Danny has done a lot of diving in his spare time."

"We're headed for an island," Dixie continued. "One that Brad Simmons has been telling the most wonderful things about. He says it has absolutely fabulous places to dive and take underwater pictures. It's got me so excited, I can scarcely wait until we get there."

Kay Orlis glanced up and saw Brad Simmons slouching indolently in the corner.

"This Mr. Simmons," she said softly, "seems to be different from the others of your party. Danny and I were surprised that a man like that would be with you."

There was a moment's silence.

"I know what you mean," Dixie replied. It seemed to Kay that words were being chosen carefully. "Actually we met Mr. Simmons a couple of weeks ago in Belize. Jess Prescott got acquainted with him, and when he offered to guide us to this island he described, we decided to take him with us.

Kay's forehead became wrinkled.

"Do you consider it safe to pick up with a stranger that way?" Kay asked. "Unknown, he might be a–a criminal or most anything."

"Oh, Jess checked on that," Dixie answered confidently. "He said liquor had made Brad what he is. He's quit his drinking and is trying to rebuild his life."

Kay waited.

"He is an experienced diver," Dixie concluded. "I can tell just by talking with him."

CHAPTER 3

CHANGES IN PERSONNEL

Mrs. Hale called dinner so they all filed into the dining room. The twins must have been waiting just outside the door. The moment the others were called, they burst in.

"Hey!" Matt exclaimed, "we're not too late, are we?"

"What chance would anyone have of sneaking to a table without you guys knowing about it?" Danny said good-naturedly.

"Matt," Mrs. Hale said, with mock hurt in her voice, "did you think I'd miss calling you, my old pals?"

"No, Aunt Wilma, but I know Danny and Uncle Mel. It's the sort of a trick they'd try."

"To get back at you for all the tricks you've pulled on us," Melvin Hale put in. "If Danny and I spent all our time at it, we still couldn't get even."

The twins were quiet for a moment and then snickered.

"We have pulled some good ones at that," Mark said.

"Let's forget the tricks now," Mrs. Hale said. "You boys come back here. I've fixed you a table all to yourselves."

"Cool!" Mark exclaimed, "we're right next to the kitchen, easy for seconds!"

"Listen to them," Danny said. "We haven't even started to eat and they're talking about seconds."

The adults gathered at the big table. Brad Simmons took his place beside Danny Orlis. The others moved to sit down but he took a step backward to count the group.

"Thirteen!" he pronounced, his eyes widening. "Thirteen! No sir, ol' Brad Simmons ain't sittin' down to no table where there's thirteen."

The Maxwell twins and Gil Adrian stared.

Melvin Hale smiled.

"Surely you're not that superstitious, Brad!" he said.

"It ain't superstition," Brad Simmons countered. "It's just plain, ordinary common sense. Thirteen brings the worst kind of bad luck."

Matt Maxwell snorted, then buried his mouth in both hands. Brad glanced at Matt, glowering.

"You know where that superstition originated, don't you?" Mel Hale asked. "At the last supper Christ had with His disciples there were thirteen at the table. And Judas betrayed our Lord and later hanged himself."

"So what?" Simmons said.

"The fact that there were thirteen at the table had nothing to do with what happened," the superintendent said. "The evil, the sin that caused Judas to betray Christ was already in his heart."

Brad Simmons stood his ground.

"Just the same, I ain't eatin' at no table where there's thirteen people."

Mrs. Hale arose.

"I'll fix a tray, Mr. Simmons," she said.

"You could eat with us, Mr. Simmons," Matt said, struggling hard to keep from laughing.

"I'm goin' to the *JUANITA MIA*!" Brad Simmons informed them.

"Please don't," Mrs. Hale pleaded. "I'll fix a tray."

Simmons went into the living room and dropped heavily to a chair. He sat glaring straight ahead until Mrs. Hale brought him the tray.

When the others had finished eating, they went back into the living room. Brad Simmons had a book from the case in the corner by then and was poring over it. His tray was forgotten nearby.

"Brad," Adrian said, his voice evidencing edginess. "You haven't eaten anything after Mrs. Hale fixed you a tray."

Brad heard him, but there was no sign he did – he did not look up.

Danny Orlis read the title, *Treasure Ships*. It seemed out of character for a fellow like Brad to be interested in it.

"I don't blame you for being taken with that book," Mel Hale said genially. "When I began to read it and I began to realize that many of those ships had actually been sunk right in this very area, I couldn't lay the book down."

Brad glanced up.

"Want to know what I think of this book?" he asked insolently. "It's a lot of poppycock! I don't believe a word of it, Gov'nor. Not a word."

"It was interesting reading," Melvin Hale replied.

The guests sat down in the living room and began to talk. After a few minutes the Mission superintendent and Captain Miguel got to their feet and went off together. It happened so casually that the others scarcely noticed that they'd gone.

Almost two hours later they came back to join the little group.

"I'm sorry we were so long," Mr. Hale said, "but Miguel and I started Bible study and the first thing we knew it was almost 10 o'clock."

"That's quite all right," Mr. Adrian said. "We've had a most enjoyable evening visiting with these young men." He indicated Danny Orlis and Mr. Maxwell.

They talked on for a time, then Mr. Adrian glanced at his watch.

"It's after 10:30," he said as he stood. "We have a big day ahead of us tomorrow."

The others followed his example, thanking the Hales for the dinner and a pleasant evening.

"It's been so good to have had a chance to visit with another girl," Dixie said to Kay. "It's been fun."

"I've enjoyed it, too," Kay Orlis told her, smiling warmly. "Only the time was so short."

"I almost wish I could stay with you until they get back," Dixie said softly.

At the door Wilbur Adrian turned to Captain D'Armando.

"Are you going to the boat now, Captain?" he asked.

Miguel stared at him questioningly.

Mr. Hale quickly translated to Spanish for him.

"No," he said, shaking his head. "Later I come by the *JUANITA MIA*."

When the last of the visitors left the house Melvin Hale turned to Danny.

"Captain D'Armando and I have something to talk over with you and Kay," the Mission superintendent said.

They turned to the rattan chairs and sat down.

"*Sí*," Captain D'Armando added. "*Sí*, we want to talk with you."

"Now Danny," Mel began, "before I go into this with you, I want you to know that it's highly irregular. It certainly isn't a part of the policy of our mission."

He paused. "Let's see, how long has it been since you and Kay have had a vacation?"

Danny thought before answering.

"Over a year," he said. "Yes, I'm sure it has been."

"That's just what I was thinking," Mr. Hale went on. "Have you any plans for taking a vacation soon?"

Danny shook his head.

"Frankly, Mel," he said, "we don't feel we can spare the money."

The Mission superintendent took a pencil from his pocket and held it thoughtfully.

"Captain D'Armando has a problem, Danny," he said, reverting to Spanish. "The boy in his crew who used to interpret for him when he had English-speaking guests charter his boat quit unexpectedly, and he didn't have time to replace him. The only person aboard who can speak Spanish and English is Brad Simmons."

"I see," Danny Orlis answered in Spanish. "That does make for a real problem. You could never be sure he was actually translating what was said."

"Exactly!" Captain D'Armando exclaimed. "Exactly! I do not trust such a one."

"What would you like to have us do?" Danny asked.

"Would you consider going with D'Armando for a couple of weeks and act as interpreter?" Melvin Hale asked.

"And maybe from the Bible teach to the men in my crew," Miguel added, "and to Miguel."

He paused.

"I try to tell them what the Bible say, but she is so hard for me. So very hard."

"The captain won't be able to pay you," Mel Hale went on, "but the cruise will cost you nothing, and it should afford you and Kay just the rest you need."

Danny Orlis turned to his young wife.

"What do you think, Kay?" he asked.

"It sounds wonderful," she said, "if you think it's all right for us to leave our work here for that long, Melvin."

"You would have to leave your work if you were going on a vacation," he said. "I think this is a good opportunity for you to get a little time off from routine here and still be able to serve Christ by instructing Miguel in the Bible between times and talk with his crew about salvation, to say nothing of doing the interpreting for him."

"You go?" Captain D'Armando asked anxiously. "You will go with Miguel?"

"*Sí*," Danny answered. "*Sí*, we go with you, if it is all right with *Señor* Adrian."

The boat captain took Danny's hand impulsively and shook it with great vigor.

"It is all right with him," he said. "I guarantee."

* * *

Kay stayed at the Hale home while the men went down to the *JUANITA MIA* to talk with Mr. Adrian. Melvin and Danny explained the situation.

"And so," Mr. Hale concluded, "Captain D'Armando would like to have Danny and Kay join your party to act as interpreter and carry on the Bible study. However, we didn't want to do it unless we have your permission."

Adrian was silent for two or three minutes.

"I have no objection," he said at last. "I'm sure none of the others will, except perhaps Brad Simmons. It doesn't matter what he thinks." He smiled. "I think that would be fine," he added, "only there is one favor I would like to ask in return. My boy was quite taken with the twins. Do you think it would be possible for the twins to join us? Gil can then have some company."

"We'd have to talk with their parents," Mr. Hale said, "but with Danny and Kay to look after them I'm sure they would be agreeable."

Back in the Hale home Mel turned to Danny and Kay. "I'm so glad you are going with Miguel," he said. "He puts in at every little port in Central America. He's got the courage it takes to speak out for Christ wherever he goes. Those two weeks you spend with him can be a real help in making him a more effective witness."

"I've been thinking about the people on board the boat, too," Kay said. "We might be able to speak often with them if we watch our opportunities and pray faithfully about it. From what I've seen and heard I doubt that any of them know Christ as a personal Savior."

They were about to leave when Melvin Hale rose and went to the bookcase.

"Wilma," he said suddenly. "Did you see that book Brad Simmons was reading, the one about treasure ships?"

She shook her head.

"Isn't it in the bookcase?" she asked.

He looked hurriedly.

"It's not here," he said.

"Do you suppose he deliberately took it?" Danny asked, giving voice to the question uppermost in each mind.

CHAPTER 4

ALL ABOARD!

On the way back to their little cottage, Danny Orlis turned to Kay.

"Well," he said, "when we went to Mel and Wilma's this evening, I certainly didn't think we would be leaving here in the morning on the *JUANITA MIA* for a two weeks' cruise."

"Neither did I," Kay answered. She shivered involuntarily.

"What's the matter?" Danny asked. "Don't you want to go?"

"Of course I do," Kay said quickly. "Only–"

"Only what?" he insisted.

"Nothing."

"Kay," Danny said, his voice growing somewhat stern. "What is it?"

"I suppose I'm just being silly," she said, "but I

can't help it. I feel a little concerned about being in the same group Brad Simmons is in."

"I can understand that," Danny replied. "He's probably harmless, but he's sure strange. He makes me want to keep my hand on my wallet."

"Danny," Kay went on. "Why would he want to take that book? All he'd have had to do was ask to borrow it and Mel would have consented."

"Perhaps he didn't take the book," Danny said. "When Mel mentioned what he was reading, Brad said it was no good and he didn't believe any of it."

"But he also told you he would not come to Hales' for dinner," Kay countered. "He came anyway. And that business about not eating with us because there were thirteen there–" She shivered again. "He gives me the creeps."

Danny laughed.

"Don't let it get you down, Kay," he said. "We've agreed to spend the next two weeks on the same boat, you know."

"Let me clue you in, Danny," she said. "When I think about Brad Simmons, I can't help wondering whether we made a mistake."

They packed some of their things that night, then got up early the next morning to finish. They were ready by the time one of the crew came to the door.

"Captain Miguel, he sent me," the dark-haired young man said in Spanish, "to help with suitcases."

"*Sí,*" Danny answered. "They are ready."

When they went down to the dock the crew was standing by to cast off. Melvin and Wilma Hale were there waiting to say goodbye to them.

"And God bless you," they said, shaking hands with them. "We'll be remembering you in prayer."

"Thanks," Danny said.

Mark and Matt Maxwell came hurrying to the *JUANITA MIA*, lugging duffel bags. Mr. and Mrs. Maxwell were coming along behind them.

"Uh, oh," Danny said when he saw them. "Here comes trouble, Kay."

The boys snorted.

"Mom and dad said we just had to go," Mark told Danny. "They said someone had to look after you."

Gil Adrian heard them on the dock and came dashing down to meet them.

"Hi Matt, Mark!" he said excitedly. "Dad was telling me that maybe you guys would get to come along."

"Yeah," Mark answered. "They had an awful time talking us into it, but we finally agreed. Someone has to take care of Danny."

"Come aboard," Gil continued. "I'll show you your cabin. You can bunk with me."

"Wait a minute," their mother called to the twins as they started aboard. "Aren't you going to say goodbye?"

They turned back.

"Now, boys, be careful," she said. In spite of herself there was a quaver in her voice.

"We will," they both promised seriously.

"And mind Danny and Kay," Dad Maxwell said. "If it weren't that Danny and Kay are going, we wouldn't let you go. You know that, don't you?"

"Don't worry," Danny put in. "They'll do as we ask. I'm not concerned about that. Kay and I will look after them."

Mrs. Maxwell turned to the boys.

"Do you have your toothbrushes?" she asked.

"Sure, Mom," they chorused.

"And your Bibles?"

"We put them in the first thing," Mark assured her. "We'll keep up with our devotions, too, the way we do at home."

Their parents quit talking so the boys said good-bye and scampered aboard.

"Do you s'pose we'll get to do some diving?" Mark asked on the way to their cabin.

"We've got plenty of gear," Gil said. "Maybe they'll let us. Have you ever tried it?"

"No," Mark said, "but I'd sure like to."

"I'll tell you what," Matt said. "You guys can do the skin diving. I'll stay on deck and watch out for sharks."

Gil Adrian's eyes opened wide.

"Watch for sharks?" he echoed. "Now what good would that do us if you were on deck watching?"

"It wouldn't do you any good," Matt continued. "That would be so I could tell our parents what happened to you."

Gil Adrian spoke soberly. "Maybe I–I won't do any diving after all."

"You can't pay attention to Matt," Mark said disdainfully. "He's just trying to scare us."

Danny and Kay again assured the Maxwells they would look out for the twins, then went aboard.

Brad Simmons was leaning against a bulkhead. His face was still clean-shaven. Except for that, no one would have recognized him as having attended the dinner at Hales' the night before.

He was back in greasy white clothes, and the same insolence gleamed in his eyes. His hair was rumpled and uncombed and stuck out carelessly in every direction from under his battered cap. For a minute he stared at Danny.

"Mornin', Gov'nor," he said. "I didn't really look for a preacher like you to be shippin' with us."

"Hello, Brad," Orlis said, striving to keep anger from his voice. "We certainly didn't expect to be here. We made up our minds at the last minute when Captain D'Armando invited us."

"Welcome aboard," Brad Simmons continued. "I'm right glad you're a-shippin' with us. You and me might b'come real friends 'fore this voyage is over. But what's the trouble, Gov'nor? Ain't the soul-savin' business what it's cracked up to be?" He laughed. "Or have you got a little larceny in your heart like all the rest of us?"

The man's manner was infuriating. Danny prayed for strength to keep his temper.

"As a matter of fact," Orlis answered, keeping his voice low, "Kay and I have come along at the captain's invitation to hold Bible study for his crew."

The look on Brad's face did not change.

"Now ain't that just ducky?" he asked, leering at them. "Outside of a trusting fella like me, who else do you figure is goin' to swallow a yarn like that?"

His laughter sounded above the drone of the engines.

"I'll clue you on somethin', Gov'nor," he went on. "You'd better come up with a better one than that if you expect to fool anyone."

"I'm not interested in fooling anyone," Danny repeated. "It happens to be the truth."

Captain D'Armando barked a sharp command. The men handling the lines leaped into action, and the *JUANITA MIA* backed slowly away from the dock.

Danny and Kay were still standing waving to their friends left on shore when Dixie Adrian came up.

"Hello!" she called happily. "I didn't know until just now that you were going to be aboard, Kay. This is going to be fun."

"We haven't known about it very long ourselves. Actually, we decided so quickly after Captain D'Armando asked us, that my head is still swimming. I didn't know it was possible to get ready in such a hurry. I was standing here now wondering if I'd forgotten anything."

"If you have," Dixie said, "you can borrow from me. Dad says I've brought along everything I own."

It was a beautiful day for sailing and the *JUANITA MIA* made good time. Somehow it seemed cooler on board than back at the Mission, and Danny and Kay reveled in it.

The twins were everywhere. Danny only spotted them once or twice all day.

The boys must have wangled the cook out of a lunch in the galley at noon, for they were nowhere around the dining saloon. At dinner that evening Captain D'Armando seated them with Danny, Kay, Dixie Adrian, and Stan Wheeler.

"Now you guys are really going to have to behave," Danny said. "You're here where I can keep an eye on you."

"Aw, Danny," Mark said, "you know we always behave."

"Hi," Stan Wheeler said. "We've hardly had a chance to get acquainted since we met."

"That's right," Danny answered, "but there ought to be plenty of time in the next week or two."

"You got acquainted with Dixie real quick-like," Mark turned to Stan.

Dixie's cheeks tinged with color.

"What makes you say that?" Stan asked.

"You helped her get seated and everything," Matt put in.

Gil Adrian snorted.

"Dixie's got a boyfriend," he said. "I think that

was why Dad brought her on this trip – so she'd forget him, maybe."

His sister flushed scarlet.

"Gilbert Adrian!"

"It's the truth," he blurted, turning to the twins. "You should see her when the phone rings. You've got to be on your toes, I tell you. When she charges forward to her phone she'd pulverize anything that got in her way!"

"Gil!" she exclaimed desperately.

"You ought to listen when she's talking to her 'so cute!' guy" he went on. "Is it mushy!"

"Gilbert Adrian!" she repeated darkly, "if I ever catch you listening, I'll–"

Gil shrugged his shoulders.

"See what I mean?"

The boat captain came over just then to Danny. "You will ask the blessing for the food?" he asked in Spanish.

Danny stood up.

"Captain D'Armando has asked me to return thanks before the food is served," he said.

Brad Simmons and Lars Krotter glared at him. Nevertheless, Lars bowed his head before Danny began to pray. Not Brad. He leaned back in his chair and stared at Danny Orlis, a sneer on his face.

CHAPTER 5

"STRING WITH ME, OR NOT?"

Matt, Mark, and Gil talked as they ate. Dixie's complexion returned to normal.

"Stan is as excited about diving," she said to Danny, "as I am about taking underwater pictures. We can hardly wait."

Danny turned to the guy on his right.

"That's interesting," he said. "Have you had experience as a diver?"

"I've done a little of it back home," Stan Wheeler admitted, "but I'm not real good at it."

"I got started back at the Angle," Danny said, "but I've done most of my diving since we've been down here."

Stan's face took on a sober cast.

"I like to dive," he said, "but I've had a lot of questions in my mind about diving down here."

"What sort?" Orlis asked.

"To tell you the truth," Stan went on, "I'm a little concerned about diving where there are sharks and barracuda."

"They aren't as much of a problem to a diver as some of the other things a guy has to face when he goes under the water around here," Danny answered.

The other boy leaned forward.

"Like what?" he asked.

"Fire coral, for one thing," Danny said. "Of course, if you wear a rash guard or wetsuit when you dive, you'll have all the protection you need."

Others had finished eating and had gone up on deck or to the lounge, but Brad Simmons was sitting staring at the two young couples at the next table.

"Well," Kay said after a time, "I think I'll go below and put up my hair."

"I'll go with you," Dixie responded.

Danny turned to Stan.

"Let's go up on deck," he said. "I'm not ready to go to our cabin."

"Good idea," his companion answered. "I want to find out more about diving."

They left the dining saloon and went to the deck.

"I'm curious," Danny began. "How did you happen to choose this particular island we're heading for?"

Stan snorted.

"That's some of my uncle's doing," he said. "His and Brad Simmons' doing."

Danny ran his fingers through his hair.

"Why that place?" he persisted. "Actually, we're passing up miles and miles of water as good for diving and underwater picture taking as we'll find where we're headed. The fishing is better really."

Stan was silent for a time.

"I wish I knew," he continued. "They keep saying it's so we'll have a better place to do diving. At first I believed it, but now I can't buy that. There has to be some other reason. They aren't that concerned about Dixie and me."

"What other reason could there be?" Danny Orlis asked.

Stan shook his head. "Now you've got me," he said. "I've thought and thought, but I haven't been able to come up with a thing."

Danny remained silent for several minutes. He stared out into the black, uninviting water.

Later the moon would be up to soften the darkness and cast a wide, shimmering beam across the waves. Now they were wrapped in shadows.

Stan seemed to have given up on diving. For a time he just stood beside Danny. Then he turned.

"I think I'll be going down to my cabin, Danny," he said. "See you in the morning."

Danny remained at the railing alone for several minutes after his companion left. Footsteps approached him in the darkness and, "Orlis?" a harsh voice demanded.

Danny started.

"What's the matter, Gov'nor?" Brad asked, laughing. "Did I scare you?"

"Not necessarily," Orlis answered, his voice firm, "I just didn't expect anyone."

Brad moved up beside him.

"I always figgered there wasn't no difference b'tween a preacher and an ordinary guy," he said contemptuously.

"I suppose you have reason for saying that," Danny replied without raising his voice.

"Now don't be so high 'n' mighty," Brad told him. "You sure didn't waste no time lettin' a little larceny crowd in on your precious Christianity."

"I don't believe I follow you," Danny said evenly.

"Now don't be givin' me that." Brad Simmons was raspy. "You might fool the rest of them, but you can't fool Brad Simmons. I'm on to you, I am."

"You're talking in riddles, Simmons," Danny Orlis said. "I don't get you at all."

Brad stepped closer and glanced over his shoulder in the darkness, as though to make sure they were alone.

"It's lucky for you I need help," Brad went on. " 'Cause I don't have no dealings with preachers. I'm goin' to let you in on a little deal."

Danny Orlis listened.

"These guys came down to fish and dive, maybe," the man went on. "They've got bit by the bug an' they've got it bad. They're really after treasure now."

He lowered his voice to a coarse whisper, "They're after gold. Gold!"

Danny turned the matter over in his mind.

"I don't think I buy that, Brad," he said slowly. "If they were after gold, they wouldn't try to keep us from knowing it. They should know we'd find out sooner or later. Why would they want to keep it from us now?"

"To beat us out of our share!" Brad snarled. "But they ain't goin' to do it! Not as long as ol' Brad Simmons is around!"

"I still can't believe it," Danny answered.

"Listen," Brad countered. "Who do you think snitched the book on treasure ships last night?"

Orlis did not answer.

"I know what you thought," Brad went on, "You figgered it was me. But I never done it." He drew himself up haughtily. "If you want to find Hale's book, slip down in Lars Krotter's room first chance you get. He keeps it hid between the mattress and the springs."

"Lars Krotter!" Danny exclaimed. "How do you know?"

"Ha!" Brad snorted scornfully. "I make it a point to know everything that goes on aboard. Now, are you goin' to string with me, or not?"

"In what?" Orlis asked.

"Do I have to spell it out?" Simmons demanded. "You and me is the divers! The kid don't count. It's you an' me has to go down and get the stuff! We've got 'em right where we want 'em! They can't make a move without us!"

There followed a long, painful silence.

"How 'bout it, Gov'nor?" Brad demanded. "I ain't got a month for you to make up your mind. Do you string along, or no?"

Orlis breathed deeply.

"I'm a guest on the *JUANITA MIA*," he said. "So are you. I couldn't take advantage of kindness by double crossing."

Brad snorted.

"If you don't look out for yourself, Buster," he said, "there ain't nobody goin' to do it for you."

"I'm sorry," Danny said, "but I'm not going to help. Even if I wanted to do it, which I don't, as a Christian I couldn't."

For a long minute Simmons was silent. Although it was too dark to see, Danny knew Brad was glaring at him.

"All right!" Brad exploded with a curse. "If I have to, I go it alone! But I want you to know this much! I ain't lettin' you or no one else stop me! Understand?"

"Are you trying to scare me?" Danny asked.

Brad took a step closer.

"I'm just warnin' you, Gov'nor," he said. "And if you're smart you'll pay 'tention. You'll pay real good 'tention."

When Danny Orlis was alone Mark Maxwell crept stealthily out of the darkness behind him. The boy moved so quietly Danny did not even know he was there until he spoke.

"Danny!" he whispered. "Danny!"

Danny Orlis turned quickly. Although he recognized Mark's voice it startled him.

"Mark!" he exclaimed. "What are you doing here?"

The boy held his finger to his lips in warning.

"S-s-sh," he cautioned. "He might still be around."

"What are you talking about?" Danny demanded.

"Brad Simmons," Mark said. "We saw him trying to get into your cabin this afternoon."

"Are you sure?" Danny asked.

"He claimed he'd made a mistake and was at the wrong door," Mark continued. "We know better, so we've been tailing him."

Danny expelled a breath sharply.

"You've been what?"

"We've been tailing him," Mark repeated. "Matt's following him now."

Danny put his hand on the boy's shoulder. "I appreciate what you're doing," he said. "It's fine for you to keep your eyes open, but you'd better drop this tailing business. It can get you into real trouble."

The silence was short and poignant.

"You–you mean we're not supposed to tail Brad?" Mark repeated.

"Right."

"But Danny," he went on, defensively. "You just can't trust that guy. He's got to be watched."

"Suppose you leave Brad Simmons to me," Orlis said.

They started to walk along the deck together.

"Danny," Mark said seriously after a minute or two, "you aren't going to help Brad with any scheme of his, are you?"

"Don't you know me any better than that?" Orlis asked gently. "I'm a Christian, Mark. I'm not going to get mixed up in anything with a man like Brad."

"I know," Mark told him, "but Matt, Gil, and me are going to have a meeting as soon as we get back to the cabin and I'm going to have to make a report. I just wanted you to say you weren't going to help him so I could tell Gil."

"Maybe it would be better for you to forget our conversation," Danny said. "Gil might tell his dad and give him the wrong impression."

"I've got to make my report," Mark said. "I promised the guys. You don't have to worry. We aren't going to tell anyone anything, at least not now."

"Why don't you make reports to me if you find something that seems important," Orlis suggested. "Then we'll decide together what to do."

"It's a deal!" Mark said, shaking Danny's hand.

"And you get hold of those friends of yours," Danny continued. "Call off this following Brad Simmons. If he'd ever find out what you're doing, Mark, he'd be so furious he might hurt one of you."

"Okay," Mark said reluctantly, "but I still think it's not fair."

CHAPTER 6

DELAYED BREAKFAST AND GOOD REASON

When Danny Orlis finally went below, Dixie had already left Kay for her own cabin.

"I was beginning to worry a little about you, Danny," Kay told him. "When we left I didn't think you were going to stay out so long."

"You'd be surprised at everything that's been going on up there tonight," he said, sitting down. "Everyone wanted to talk to me."

"Who, for instance?"

"Brad Simmons," he said, "and Mark."

"Mark!" she echoed. "What was he doing up there? He should have been in bed."

"Mark and Matt were trailing Simmons," Danny related.

"But why?" she asked.

"They think he's a suspicious character," Danny

said. A smile crossed his face. "Fortunately Brad didn't get onto them. I get the cold chills thinking what would have happened if he had. I've put a stop to it."

Kay moistened her lips.

"I almost wish we had stayed at the Mission," she said. "I know I shouldn't feel as I do about Brad Simmons, but I can't help it, Danny. I think I've never had anyone affect me quite as he does."

"He's not a very desirable person," Danny replied. "I'll have to go along with you on that, but I think we need not be afraid of him."

He told her what had taken place.

Kay Orlis's eyes looked far away and for a time she did not speak.

"Do you believe it, Danny?" she asked. "I mean about Mr. Krotter stealing that book and about Dixie's dad and the others being after gold?"

Danny sat down and rubbed his chin.

"I don't know what to believe," he said. "To tell you the truth, Kay, they all act nice enough when we talk with them, but you can't tell what one will do when there's money involved. Did Dixie say anything to give you a clue as to what she thought about the trip? Anything that might lead you to believe she considered it something besides a vacation?"

"No," Kay replied, "not that I can recall." Suddenly her expression changed.

"Wait a minute!" she exclaimed. "She did make a remark or two. She said she'd been looking forward to having so much fun diving and taking pictures in the water. Now that they were about to get to the place, she wasn't so sure it would be the fun she had expected."

"Did she say why?" Danny asked.

Kay shook her head. "No, and she made the remark so casually I didn't really notice it."

"There's one thing that causes a question mark as far as I'm concerned," Danny said. "Any way you think of it, it doesn't make sense."

"What's that?" Kay asked.

"The way everyone talks, Brad Simmons is the one who convinced Adrian and his pals to visit this island. If that's true, how could *they* be seriously hunting treasure?"

"I still don't follow you," Kay put in.

"Well, look at it this way." Danny Orlis was talking partly with his hands. "If Brad Simmons picked out the place we are to go to dive, how could Adrian, Krotter, and Prescott be after treasure? You don't just drop anchor anywhere and start diving for gold bullion. You've got to find the place first. There isn't a chance in a million that there would be treasure where Simmons is directing them."

"Unless–" Kay broke in.

"Unless what?"

"Unless Brad Simmons is taking us to a place where there is treasure," Kay said.

Danny thought about that for a moment or two.

"Why would he do that? If he knew the place

where the treasure was, why wouldn't he go and get it? Then he wouldn't have to worry about sharing."

"That," Kay answered laughing, "is for you to figure out."

Danny walked slowly across the little cabin and back again.

"Somehow this thing has to fit together," he said. "But how?"

Next morning when he and Kay went on deck on their way to breakfast, they saw a small island in the distance.

"I suppose that's the place where we're headed," Danny observed.

Before Kay could say anything, Captain D'Armando came hurrying over.

"*Señor*," he said, "it is not so long until we are at the destination. Then it is much work for everyone."

"Could we have the Bible studies now, before breakfast? If we wait, it is maybe too late today."

"Certainly," Danny answered. "Get the men together in your cabin. I'll go for my Bible and be right with you."

"Could we give it two times?" Miguel asked. "Then the men on duty can be relieved so they can hear."

There were only four men and the captain in the cabin where Danny and Kay held the Bible study. The men listened attentively and broke in often with questions. Captain D'Armando's eyes were shining when Danny Orlis finished.

"One moment!" Miguel exclaimed. "One moment and I get the others!" He turned to the members of the crew. "Quick!" he ordered. "Take your places so the rest may come!"

He went to take the wheel so the first mate could be relieved for Bible study.

Danny and Kay repeated the session. The result was the same as with the first group. The men were attentive and eager to learn.

The young missionaries had started to breakfast before 7 o'clock. Now, more than two hours later they were going to the dining saloon to eat.

"Wasn't that wonderful?" Kay asked. "Such an attentive audience!"

"Miguel has been talking to them," Danny said. "Those men have heard the gospel before. It was easy to see that."

"They have heard the gospel," Kay acknowledged, "and what is more important, they have seen the gospel demonstrated in Miguel's life."

"You can say that again," Danny said fervently. "Knowing him is like hearing a sermon."

Brad Simmons passed them. His eyes met Danny's. Hostility was undisguised.

Kay and Danny had just sat down when the twins and Gil Adrian came to the doorway. They whispered together, then filed inside and trooped to the table where Danny and Kay were sitting.

"Danny," Mark said, keeping his voice low. "We'd like to talk with you."

"Okay," Danny said.

They stood there, waiting.

"We'd like to talk to you alone," Mark added.

"Now listen, guys," Orlis said, "you can talk in front of Kay. I don't have secrets from Mrs. Orlis."

The boys looked from one to the other.

"Are you sure we can trust her to keep quiet?" Gil put in.

"Sure thing," Orlis assured them.

"I won't tell anything," Kay said.

"Danny," Mark went on. "You told us not to follow Brad Simmons, and we don't want to do something you don't want us to do, but would you please change your mind? Would you let us trail him?"

"We'll promise not to get caught," Matt added.

Orlis shook his head. "I'm sorry guys," he said, "there's not a chance."

The boys could not hide their disappointment.

"See, I told you it wouldn't do any good," Mark said.

"All right," Gil said, resignation in his voice. "We won't tail him, but I can tell you this. This detective job is like going hunting without ammunition."

The three left the dining saloon.

Gil's sister met them outside the door.

"Now what was the matter with them?" she asked as she came in and approached the table where Danny and Kay were sitting at breakfast.

"They're disappointed because I vetoed a little project of theirs," Danny answered.

"I've been looking all over for you," Dixie Adrian said, changing the subject. "What happened? Did you oversleep?"

"No," Kay said. "We've been in the captain's cabin, having Bible study for him and for members of his crew."

Dixie frowned.

"Bible study?" she echoed, wrinkling her nose.

"It was amazing," Kay continued, "I don't know when we've had a more attentive group."

"But Kay," Dixie protested, "they're all–they're all *natives*."

"In the eyes of the Lord Jesus, they are souls that will go into eternity lost, without hope, unless we bring them His glorious message of salvation," Kay answered simply.

Dixie straightened, then smiled.

"I think I'll sit here while you eat if you don't mind. I'm so excited I'm about to burst!"

"What's brought that on?" Danny asked.

She paused and looked around. Sure there was no one else in the room, she leaned forward and lowered her voice.

"I don't think it will hurt to tell you," she said. "You'll be finding it out soon enough."

"If it's something you've promised not to tell," Danny said, "perhaps you shouldn't."

"It isn't that," Dixie whispered. "It's just that there are certain people aboard that they don't want to find out about this until the last minute."

Something in her manner caused the little dining saloon to seem close and stifling hot to Danny.

"I see," he said.

Kay was listening intently.

"Dad and Lars thought it strange that Brad Simmons was awfully anxious about getting to this particular island," she went on. "They knew it wasn't because he wanted to find us a good place to go diving and take pictures."

"That's right," Danny observed. "A guy like that one doesn't do anything for anyone unless it's going to do him some personal good."

"That's what Dad said," Dixie reported.

"Then at Mr. Hale's the other night, Lars happened to see the place where Brad was reading in the book, *Treasure Ships*."

"So Mr. Krotter picked it up when he left," Danny finished, "and took it with him."

She stared incredulously.

"How did you know?" she asked.

He only smiled. For the moment he had decided to tell her nothing more than she already knew.

"He wasn't going to steal that book, Danny," Dixie protested. "He was going to take it to Mr. Hale himself and explain what happened or have you take it."

Danny nodded.

"He and Dad have been studying the book ever since," she said. "They are sure they've found the reason Brad was so anxious to get over to the island. It wasn't to show us a good time, and it wasn't just so he'd get transportation to the island."

The steward came in with more coffee. Dixie waited until he had gone before continuing.

"They figure," she said hoarsely, "that Brad knows there's a ship with treasure sunk off the coast of the island!"

Kay opened her mouth to speak, but Danny stopped her with a look.

"Are you sure?" Orlis asked.

"As sure as you can ever be about a person like Brad."

"How do they think he planned to get to it?" Danny asked. "Or to bring it up, if he did find it? The gold, I mean."

"That's something they don't know," Dixie answered.

Jess Prescott appeared at the door to the dining saloon.

Dixie's face colored and she put her finger to her lips.

"Don't say a word!" she whispered. "We're not sure we can trust him! He's the one who insisted we take Brad Simmons along!"

CHAPTER 7

WHAT OF CARTER'S REEF?

Down in their cabin the Maxwell twins and Gil Adrian met for a whispered consultation.

"Is the door locked?" Mark asked.

"I double checked," Matt answered.

They went to the bunks and sat down. For a moment or two no one spoke.

"Well," Matt began, "what do you think now?"

"I haven't changed my mind," Gil Adrian said. "Brad Simmons is up to something. I don't care what Danny Orlis says. I think we ought to follow him."

"Oh, no," the twins spoke quickly. "Danny told us not to do it."

"We've got to keep watch on Brad," Gil protested. "If we don't, we're not going to find out what he's planning."

"Just the same we can't trail him," Mark said firmly.

"What's it going to hurt?" Gil demanded. "He won't need to know a thing about it."

"We're Christians, Gil," Mark explained. "And we promised before we left home that we would do what Danny tells us."

Gil stared at them in disgust.

"I don't get you guys at all," he said. "You act as though you're okay, but every night you have to read your Bible and pray. Now, when it means everything to us to find out what Simmons is doing, you won't help at all just because Danny asked you." He got up and shrugged his shoulders. "I don't get it."

"We feel as badly as you do about it," Mark said. "Remember, I was the one who suggested tailing Brad Simmons in the first place. A Christian is supposed to keep his word. We can't do differently."

Gil sat down.

"I never did see anybody as goofy over religion as you guys," he said in disgust.

"It isn't that," Matt answered. "Religion is something men have thought up."

"And being Christian," Mark added, "is something a lot different. A Christian has accepted Jesus as his Savior and with His help tries to follow Him."

"It still doesn't make sense to me," Gil countered.

"Well, it's this way," Mark went on. "The Bible tells us that we're all wicked and none of us are fit to go to heaven, so God sent Jesus to earth. He died on the cross and came to life again so we can be saved."

The corners of Gil's mouth tightened up.

"How?" he asked.

"By knowing we are sinners and that we need a Savior," Matt told him. "By putting our faith in the Lord Jesus Christ to save us."

"I sure wouldn't want to do that," Gil answered after a time. "A guy never could have any fun."

"That's where you're wrong," the boys both said in unison. "We have great times. You don't know how happy you can be until you're a Christian."

Gil Adrian squirmed uncomfortably.

"I don't care what you do," he said, changing the subject abruptly. "I'm going to tail Brad Simmons!"

* * *

The *JUANITA MIA* reached the island while Danny, Kay, and Dixie were still in the dining saloon. The throbbing engines quieted, and the boat slowed. Dixie Adrian looked from Danny to Kay. Her eyes shone with excitement and anticipation.

"Don't say a word to anyone about the things I've just told you," she whispered.

"You can depend on us," Danny assured her.

They got up and went out on deck. Now that the boat had all but stopped, the stifling heat closed in about them.

Brad Simmons was standing at the railing near the prow, staring with seeming laziness out across the water. He looked as though he were all but asleep. However, at the sound of footsteps he straightened and turned Danny's way with deliberation, his face showing a taunting sneer. Orlis realized suddenly that Brad had been waiting for him all the time.

The dark-haired soldier of fortune stared at Danny. Then he sidled up to him.

"Can I talk with you a minute, Gov'nor?" he demanded coolly.

Because he could think of no way to avoid it, Orlis followed Brad a few steps to one side.

"What is it?" he asked, making no attempt to keep his voice down.

Simmons glanced about quickly.

"Take it easy, Gov'nor!" he barked hoarsely. "Take it easy! Do you want the whole boat hearin' us?"

"Actually," Danny said, "it doesn't matter to me one way or another. I have nothing to hide."

"You have your chance to cut in on this deal," Brad went on in an undertone that even Danny found difficult to hear. "Are you goin' to go along or are you still goin' to be the fool?"

"I have no intention of changing my mind about stringing along with you," Danny replied. "If that's what you mean."

Wilbur Adrian came along just then.

He must have seen that Danny and Brad were in serious conversation, but there was nothing to indicate it in Adrian's manner.

"Well, Brad," he began loudly as he approached. "Here we are. Now where do you think we ought to start diving?"

The question seemed to startle Simmons. He breathed deeply, then shook his head.

"Search me, Gov'nor," he said. "Don't know as it makes a difference as long as we get in shallow water. You'll be findin' tropical fish and beautiful coral all around the island. When Stan and Dixie come up with the stories of what they've seen down there, it's goin' to make you want to start diving."

"I doubt that," Mr. Adrian answered.

Slowly Brad turned from the railing.

"Want I should go and tell the cap'n to get in among the reefs anywhere?" he asked.

Wilbur Adrian nodded carelessly. "If you think that's best, it's all right with me," Adrian said.

"It doesn't make much difference where we dive around here," Simmons said. "You're going to see the most fantastic sights you've ever seen. And after we've done a little diving, I'll take you fishing – if you want. Like I told Jess and Krotter, the fishin' around this island is fantastic."

"No wonder they were so anxious to bring you along," Wilbur Adrian replied.

Simmons laughed.

"I got my good points, Gov'nor," he said. "I got my good points."

And with that he started toward the wheelhouse. Adrian walked part way with him.

They left Danny standing alone. For a moment or two he watched Mr. Adrian and Brad Simmons. Then he turned and went down to his cabin.

* * *

After their conference below, the Maxwell twins and Gil made their way up to the deck. They passed Danny in the passageway.

"We've about stopped," Mark said as they met him. "What's happened?"

"Nothing," Danny answered. "We've just reached the place where we're going. I suppose we'll be doing a little diving after a while."

"Oh, wow!" Matt exclaimed. "I sure hope I get to try it."

"We'll have to see about that," Danny answered, "when the time comes, but don't count on it too strongly; I don't want you to be disappointed."

"That guy!" Gil snorted when Orlis was out of hearing. "Who does he think he is, anyway? He acts as though he owns you."

"Danny's all right," Matt said defensively. "If he thinks it's safe, he'll let us dive."

They went on to the deck and looked around.

"That's funny," Mark said. "I don't believe we're moving at all."

"Of course not," Gil retorted. "You heard Danny say we've reached the place where we're going, didn't you?"

Mark Maxwell nodded.

"Sure, but you'd think we would drop anchor," he said. "The boat just doesn't seem to be going anywhere, and Captain D'Armando hasn't shut off the engines."

Matt looked up.

"See who's talking to the captain?" he questioned.

"Brad Simmons!" Gil and Mark exclaimed.

The captain and Brad were standing near the wheelhouse. Brad was doing most of the talking. They could tell that. Of course they were too far away to hear anything that was being said.

"I'd sure like to know what they're talking about," Matt said.

"If you weren't so pious, we could sneak up and find out," Gil taunted. "Only we wouldn't be able to understand them. They're probably talking Spanish."

"Who wouldn't be able to understand them?" Mark asked. "We live down here. Remember? That's it!" he exclaimed in a soft whisper. "That's it!"

Matt and Gil both stared at him.

"What are you talking about?" they demanded.

"You and I can understand Spanish, Matt," he said. "I don't think Brad Simmons knows that."

"We can go up in the wheelhouse speaking English," Mark said. "Maybe they'll keep on talking."

"Sounds like a good idea," Gil replied, "but what about your precious Danny? What's he going to think if we do a thing like that?"

"He told us not to trail Brad," Mark said. "He was afraid we'd get caught and get in trouble with the guy. But this is different. There isn't anything wrong with going up in the wheelhouse just because Brad Simmons is there."

"We've gone up to the wheelhouse lots of times," Matt put in. "No one will think anything about it. Danny did tell us to keep our eyes open."

"Only this time," Mark added, "it'll be our ears."

"*Ay de mi!* I just hope we don't get 'em chopped off," his brother mumbled.

"Now that was a happy thought," Mark said.

When they were halfway to the bridge Gil grasped Matt by the arm.

"I just thought of something," he said. "You don't suppose Brad Simmons and the captain are in on this deal together, whatever it is."

The boys shook their heads. "Captain D'Armando wouldn't line up with a fellow like Brad. The captain is a Christian."

Gil looked at them quizzically.

The boys continued on their way to the wheelhouse, talking excitedly about skin diving. As they entered, the captain looked up.

"*Buenos Días,*" he said.

Mark started to answer in Spanish but caught himself just in time.

"H-hello," he stammered.

The other boys also greeted the captain in English.

Brad Simmons eyed them suspiciously.

"What are you guys doing here?" he demanded.

"Captain D'Armando doesn't care," Mark answered. "He lets us come up here."

"What is it the Americano ask you to tell me?" the captain broke in quickly.

The boys went to the front of the wheelhouse and pretended to lose themselves in studying the chart.

For an instant Brad hesitated.

"What did he say?" Miguel repeated.

"He told me to tell you they want to go to the wreckage on Carter's Reef," Brad said.

Captain D'Armando glanced at the compass, briefly calculated their position, and turned the *JUANITA MIA* almost 160 degrees. The boat turned slowly and the captain waited until she was heading in the right direction before opening the throttle.

Simmons wheeled and went striding away arrogantly.

The boys stared at one another.

"What do you suppose that meant?" Gil whispered.

Mark shook his head. "But I'll find out," he said.

He went to Captain D'Armando.

"Where are we going?" he asked in Spanish.

The captain laughed. "You already know that, Mark," he said. "You heard Simmons."

"*Sí,*" the boy answered, "but what is this wreckage? And why we go there?"

"Why we go there I do not know," he said. "The wreckage is an old ship on the reef. It can be seen at low tide. The water, she is very clear and not so deep on Carter's Reef."

The boys' eyes looked their curiosity.

"What is it?" Gil demanded excitedly in English. "What is he saying?"

Mark shook his head.

"Have you ever seen this wreckage?" he asked, "with your own eyes?"

"*Sí*," Captain D'Armando answered. "Many times, I see. She lie in the water." He motioned with his hands. "So."

"Maybe that's what all this talk about deep sea diving is about," Matt whispered in his brother's ear.

"Has anyone ever tried to dive to the wreck?" the boy continued. "To look there for gold or silver or jewels?"

Miguel's forehead wrinkled.

"You read too many pirate stories," he said. "The boys from the village, they dive to her for fun. And one time a boat come down from Cuba to see if she have anything of value aboard. The hurricane come and – pouf! She drive them on the reefs and almost kill them all. They never come back."

"*Qué terrible! Señor!*" Mark said, trying hard to keep from showing his excitement. *Qué terrible!*"

They hurried back out on deck.

"What is it?" Gil insisted. "Tell me what he said!"

"We've got to get to Danny and quick!" Mark said.

CHAPTER 8

NOW, WHERE IS THE UNDERWATER CAMERA?

The Maxwell twins and Gil Adrian found Danny and Kay in the cabin.

"Hi, guys," Danny said, opening the door. "I didn't expect to see you so soon."

Mark looked in each direction stealthily and just about crept inside. "Come on," he hissed to his companions. "Let's get in before he sees us."

"Before who sees who?" Kay asked curiously. "What's happened?"

Matt turned to Danny.

"Maybe you'd better lock the door," he whispered. "We don't want anyone to know we're here."

"Especially Brad Simmons," Gil put in.

Before Danny could turn the lock in the door there was a sharp knock.

"If that's Brad, don't let him in," Mark whispered.

The knock came again.

"Orlis!" a coarse voice called, "I got to talk to you a minute."

"It's Brad!" Mark quietly gasped.

Kay got to her feet and motioned in silence toward the closet. As Danny went to open the door, Kay shunted the twins and Gil out of sight.

"Well," Danny said, opening the door, "you didn't say anything about visiting me so soon when we talked a while ago."

"It's not my idea," Brad grunted. He remained at the door. "I just stopped to tell you Adrian wants you to go divin' right away."

"I'll be up in a little while," Danny said.

Still the man at the door did not move.

"Ain't changed your mind about throwin' in with me, have you?" he asked. "I got to have someone. It had just as well be you, preacher."

Danny shook his head.

"The answer is still the same."

Simmons laughed. "Just thought I'd ask," he said. With that he went swaggering up the passageway.

Orlis watched until he was sure Brad was gone. Then he closed the door and locked it.

"He's gone," Kay said. "You boys can come out." Matt wiped the perspiration from his forehead.

"I tell you that was close!" he exclaimed.

"When we heard Brad's voice, I thought we were goners," Gil said.

"I think that's why he came to see you," Mark observed. "He wanted to find out if we were here."

Danny grasped him gently by the shoulders.

"Now listen," he said. "Suppose you simmer down and tell us what this is all about."

"It's this way," the boy began. "Brad was up in the wheelhouse talking with Captain D'Armando."

"I know," Danny said. "I was with Gil's dad when he told Brad to tell Captain to go in among the reefs anywhere, that we were going to do some diving."

"But that's not what he told him!" Matt protested.

"How do you know what he told Captain?" Orlis asked suspiciously.

"We were there," Mark said.

"You what?" Danny demanded. His face grew stern. "I thought I told you not to follow Brad Simmons."

"We didn't," Gil said. "We figured Brad wouldn't know Matt and Mark could understand Spanish, so we just went busting into the wheelhouse and fiddled around while they were talking."

"I see."

"Brad didn't tell Captain what you said," Matt went on. "He told him that Gil's dad wanted to go to a wreck on some special reef." His forehead wrinkled. "I can't remember the name of it."

"A wreck?" Kay asked. "But why?"

Danny thought for a moment.

"Some of those old ships were carrying gold," he explained. "I can't figure why he would do that.

Surely if there were any gold aboard a ship that went down in a place where it can be seen, it would have been searched stem to stern long ago."

"That sounds reasonable to me," Kay said.

"Just the same," Mark added. "That's what he said. Captain D'Armando knew right where it was. He didn't ask the directions or anything."

"I'm going to talk with Miguel the first chance I get," Danny said. "There are so many things about this deal that don't add up."

Danny got into his rash guard and swimming trunks and went topside. They were just lowering a second small boat into the water.

"Oh, Kay!" Dixie cried. "You've just got to try it! It's the most beautiful place I've ever seen. There are the most gorgeous, tiny little fish down there, coral, and everything. You've got to see it!"

"Not today," Kay Orlis answered. "I may get up my courage, but right now I want to watch someone else."

"I just hope my pictures turn out!" Dixie went on. "I'm going to develop the black and whites as soon as we quit diving. I think these will have such a better feel than digital photos."

"I told you what it was goin' to be like, Gov'nor," Brad Simmons said boastfully to Mr. Adrian. "You listen to her. She'll make divers out of all of you before you know it."

Danny went to where Captain D'Armando was standing.

"Hey, Orlis!" Brad called from the little boat. "Are you going to dive this afternoon or aren't you?"

"I'll see you tonight, Captain," Danny whispered. "If I can manage."

"Sí."

He went down to the little skiff and cast off.

"I checked your gear," Stan Wheeler told him.

"Thanks."

Nevertheless, Danny went over the valves and hose connections carefully, one by one. It was only when he was satisfied that everything was in first class condition he put on the breathing apparatus.

"Don't you trust nobody?" Brad Simmons asked.

"Certainly," Danny said. "And I especially trust Stan. But I make no apology for inspecting diving gear I'm going to be using. Turn the wrong valve on one of these things and it can be the last mistake you'll ever make."

Although there was scorn in Brad's manner, he did have respect, too. Something he had for few men.

Danny lowered himself into the water and swam downward gracefully. There were parrot and trigger fish swimming among the coral and an occasional grouper. Sea fans and sponges and many-colored coral were everywhere! The spot was indeed beautiful, but no more beautiful than any of a hundred places on the reefs just off the Mission station.

Then Orlis saw the ship. She was lying on her side, heavily encrusted with coral. He swam over to her. She was not particularly large, even for a sailing ship, but she was very old. He could tell that by the shape. The mast had long since been broken up by the action of the waves, and there was a great, gaping hole in her superstructure. It seemed as though the ship beckoned to him irresistibly.

He would have investigated at that moment, but Stan glided down beside him. Danny hesitated. It would be better, first, to see how well Stan could handle himself in the water. The investigation would have to wait.

Brad Simmons dove with them, but he swam about, watching Dixie and helping her get the pictures she wanted. He paid so little attention to the ship it was almost as though he didn't know it was there.

When Danny finally surfaced, Wilbur Adrian and Lars Krotter were waiting for him.

"What did you see, Danny?" Wilbur asked. "What's the ship like?"

"That's hard to say," Danny answered. "She's not too large. Of course she was a sailing ship, but she's covered with coral."

"Is she a man-of-war?"

Danny shook his head.

"Couldn't tell a thing," he said. "And I want to find out just how much experience Stan Wheeler has had before I take him into a tight place."

"He's a little young," Lars answered, "but I've seen him dive. I think he can handle himself, all right."

"He didn't do too badly today," Danny said. "After we work together a little, I'll be able to know just what he can do."

"Of course," Wilbur Adrian said, "if we find anything we'll cut you in on it."

"If you'd want to donate my share to the Mission," Orlis told them, "it would be all right with me.

He paused.

"Tell me," he continued, "have you talked with Brad Simmons about the same thing?"

"We wanted to get a bit farther along, first," Adrian said, "before we mention our plans to him."

"It might be a good idea to talk with him now," Orlis suggested.

It seemed to him that both men stiffened.

"We'll decide when it's time to talk with Brad Simmons," Adrian retorted curtly.

Danny wanted to talk with Captain D'Armando right away, but when he got dressed and went up to the wheelhouse Miguel was not there.

"He is in his cabin," the first officer said. "He'll be on duty after dinner."

"Fine. I'll see him then."

Kay was waiting for Danny on deck.

"Well," she said softly, after making sure they were alone, "did you learn anything?"

"Not exactly," he said. "But I've been doing a powerful lot of thinking."

"For instance?"

"I think I've figured out why Adrian asked Brad to give instructions to Miguel," he said, "instead of having me do it."

Someone went by just then and Kay nudged Danny to silence.

"They wanted Brad to give the instructions," he went on when they were again alone, "because they knew he would direct D'Armando to the sunken ship. They knew he wouldn't take them to just any spot on the reefs."

"That makes sense," she acknowledged. "Danny, what about Brad Simmons? If he has known all along where this ship is, why hasn't he come here alone and dived to it? It seems to me he's made things unnecessarily hard for himself by bringing so many people here."

"He might have needed transportation," Danny said.

"If that's all he needed," Kay insisted, "why doesn't he now jump ship and search for the treasure on his own?"

"Probably for the same reason that he needed transportation," Orlis answered. "He's broke more than likely. He would need a ship or a large boat of some sort to use as a base of operations. No, I can see why he feels he has to stay with the *JUANITA MIA*. But I still can't understand why he doesn't want to string in with them – why they'll take us in, but not Brad."

"There are a lot of strange things about these people," Kay said. "Sometimes I wish the four of us had stayed back at the Mission."

Dinner over, Danny slipped out of the dining saloon and made his way to the bridge.

"I'm curious about this ship, Miguel," he said. "Everyone seems sure there is treasure aboard her."

"*Sí,*" Captain D'Armando said, "*Sí.*"

"But I can't understand how there could be anything worth diving for. She's in such shallow water, everybody knows she's here. Don't you think someone has gone over her thoroughly a long time ago?"

Miguel D'Armando puckered his lips.

"Maybe they do at night or early morning when the people of the village, yonder, not see them," he said. "I only can tell you of the things I know. But everyone say if there was ever gold aboard her it is there. No one has ever got it out."

"Thanks, Captain," Danny said warmly.

"And *Señor* Orlis," Miguel went on. "When you dive here, be careful."

Orlis turned back. "What do you mean?"

"Everyone say she is most dangerous," Captain D'Armando told him, "the ship below. They say more than one has been trapped and lost his life down there."

Danny nodded.

"Thanks for the information, Captain," he said. "I know these old wrecks can be tricky."

On the way below, Danny met Dixie Adrian in the passageway.

"What's the matter?" he asked. "You look worried."

"I am," she said. "Have you seen my underwater camera? I can't find it anywhere."

Danny shook his head.

"No," he answered, "but it must be around someplace. It's too large to be lost very long."

"That's what I thought," she said, "but I've looked every place I've been since noon, and it has vanished."

Danny rubbed his cheek with his forefinger.

"Everybody was excited while the diving was going on," he said. "Could it have been kicked overboard accidentally?"

"That's what Dad asked," she said, "but I know it wasn't. I distinctly remember bringing it back on the *JUANITA MIA* with me."

"That is too bad," he said. "Do you have any ideas?"

She nodded, her eyes flashing.

"If you ask me," she said, "I think it was stolen!"

CHAPTER 9

A RESTLESS NIGHT

That night Danny and Kay had their evening devotions and went to bed at the usual time, but sleep was slow in coming. For a long while they lay talking in hushed tones.

"Have you had a chance to talk to Dixie about Christ, Kay?" Danny asked.

"I've tried it several times," she answered. "For some reason she always shies away when the subject comes up. She seems to sense when I'm going to mention spiritual things and is on guard."

"I've tried to talk with her dad, too," Danny said, "and with Prescott and Lars Krotter, but I haven't had a good opportunity to present the gospel. Actually they don't seem to oppose the gospel, just are indifferent to it."

For a time they listened to the murmuring waves.

"How about Brad?" Kay asked at last.

"He's a different story," Danny said. "I've never

met anyone like him. He's bitterly antagonistic to the gospel. Every time I've even mentioned that I'm a Christian, he blows up."

They talked on longer and finally drifted off to sleep.

In the cabin down the passageway the Maxwell twins and Gil Adrian got ready for bed. Gil would have turned out the light, but Matt stopped him.

"We haven't had our Bible reading yet," he said.

"I thought I could make you forget," Gil answered.

Mark went to the desk and picked up the Bible.

"Would it be all right if we read out loud?" he asked. "We'd like to have you join us, Gil."

Gil plopped on his bunk.

"Okay," he said with resignation. "Go ahead and get it over with. It won't hurt me any."

It was Mark's turn. Gil did not know where he read, but the verses drove to the very depths of his heart.

It was what Jesus said about sheep. How the sheep knew the voice of the Shepherd and would follow Him, but they wouldn't follow a stranger.

Verily, verily, I say unto you, I am the door of the sheep.

All that ever came before me are thieves and robbers: but the sheep did not hear them.

I am the door: by me if any man enter in, he shall be saved. . . .

When Mark finished, the twins knelt to pray. Gil Adrian bowed his head and fought against the aching in his heart. As soon as they finished praying he jumped into bed and turned his back so they wouldn't talk to him.

Although Gil thought he was so tired he scarcely could stay awake another minute, when he got into bed sleep refused to come. He tossed restlessly on the narrow bunk. In a short time the twins were sleeping soundly, and that disturbed him the more. All the verses they had read came back to nag at him. He was surprised that he remembered them.

All we, like sheep, have gone astray. . . .

For all have sinned and come short of the glory of God.

The wages of sin is death, but the gift of God is eternal life through Jesus Christ, our Lord.

He rolled over and looked out the porthole. The moon was casting a mellow light over the sleeping water. Gil sighed and swung his feet over the side of the bunk.

Those Bible verses applied to him. It made no difference how hard he tried to dodge them, or how much he tried to make himself believe he was so good he didn't need to worry that he would be saved. Those verses hammered into the depths of his being. He was lost. Lost!

How long he sat on the side of his bunk he would never know. Turmoil was within him. It had surely been one hour and may have been two or three. He just sat there, motionless. The silence was broken briefly by the sound of something dropping into the water.

The noise startled Gil. He leaped to his feet; while watching he listened intently. But from that moment all was silent again.

For a time Gil did not move. Then he tiptoed across the little cabin and awakened the twins.

"Somebody dropped something overboard," he said. "I just heard it."

"What makes you think that?" Matt questioned sleepily, rubbing his eyes.

"I heard it, I tell you."

"How could you hear anything in your sleep?"

Gil hesitated.

"I–I wasn't asleep," he stammered.

"Are you sure you heard something?" Mark insisted.

"I'm positive." He crept to the porthole and peered out.

The twins got up and moved up beside him. "Can you see anything?"

Gil shook his head.

"Not a thing. But I know something dropped into the water just now. I heard it."

"Maybe we could see from up on deck," Mark suggested.

"You–you mean you plan to go out there?" Matt whispered. "Brad Simmons might be prowling around, you know."

"We could keep out of his way," Gil said. "Come on."

They slipped into dark clothes and, barefooted, moved out into the passageway.

Mark led the way to the stairs. He moved slowly, feeling his way along the narrow passage. Gil and Matt followed close behind.

"Ouch!" one of them gasped, suddenly.

Mark's blood froze. "What's wrong?" he asked, turning.

"I stubbed my toe," Gil muttered.

"Well, keep quiet," Mark ordered in a hoarse whisper. "You'll have everybody awake."

"About now I'm wishing they were awake," Matt said.

They inched their way up the steps and out on the deck. The cool night air felt good. The moon was half under a cloud, but there was light enough so they could make out almost everything on deck. Uncertainly for a moment or two they paused.

"See anything?" Gil asked.

Mark shook his head.

"Whoever was up here had plenty of time to throw whatever you heard hit the water then get back to his cabin," Matt said. "I think we'd just as well go to bed. We're not going to find anything up here."

"Maybe not," Mark replied reluctantly.

"We'd just as well look around," Gil said, "as long as we're here."

"I was afraid you'd say that," Matt retorted.

It was Gil Adrian who first noticed that the lifeboat was gone. For a time he stared at the davits where it had been suspended.

"Guys," he said at last, "there's something missing over there, but I can't think what it is."

"Lifeboat!" Mark whispered.

The boys did not move. For the moment they could not.

"Could that have been what you heard hit the water?" they asked Gil.

"I didn't think it was that big," Gil said. "I suppose it could have been."

They approached the davits reluctantly and peered over the side. The lines were still dangling from the pulleys.

"That must have been it," Matt said.

"Somebody must have left the *JUANITA MIA* this evening," Mark added.

"But why?" his brother asked.

Gil Adrian straightened.

"That," he said, "is what *we've* got to find out."

For a minute no one spoke. Standing there, they stared down into the water.

"What are we going to do?" Mark asked.

"I make a motion we go to bed," Matt said. "We're getting nowhere fast."

"Sounds like a good–" Mark's voice stopped.

"What was that?" he demanded.

The boys were staring at him.

"What was what?" they asked in unison.

"I–I saw something in the w-w-water," Mark stammered. "A flash of light!"

"Wait a minute!" Matt countered. "You sound a little batty. Are you sure you feel all right?"

"I saw a light flash in the water," Mark repeated. "If you guys had your eyes open, you'd have seen it."

"You mean *on* the water, don't you?" Gil asked.

"I mean *in* the water. Underneath."

"I believe most everything you tell me, Mark."

There it was! The light had flashed again.

"There!" Mark said quietly. "Did you see it?"

Gil and Matt nodded.

"I–I still don't know whether I can believe it," Gil said, "but I–I saw it."

"What could it be?" Mark asked.

"Oh, no!" Matt said. "I don't care how curious we are! We're not going overboard to see what that light is! That's one place where I'm saying 'no' and I mean it! No diving at this time!"

"Look over there," Gil broke in. "There's the lifeboat! There's nobody in it!"

The Maxwell twins swallowed hard.

"I–I think we'd better go a-a-and wake Danny," Matt said. "We can't handle this."

"Sounds like a good idea," Gil answered.

They left the deck and made their way, as rapidly as they could, down the stairs and through the passageway.

Matt knocked on Danny's cabin door softly, but insistently.

"Do you think we can wake him?" Mark asked, breathing heavily.

"We've got to!" Matt replied.

CHAPTER 10

THEY IDENTIFY THE MAN

Danny Orlis stirred restlessly as the sound of the knocking seeped into his subconscious. It was Kay who awakened first. She sat up in bed and listened as the knock came again.

"Danny!" she exclaimed in a low whisper. "Danny! Someone's knocking at the door!"

She reached over and pushed him.

He shook his head and rolled over.

"Danny!" she called again. This time she grasped him by the shoulder and shook him.

Her voice and the sounds at the door began to register. He sat up quickly and swung his legs over the side of the bunk. For a moment he sat groggily rubbing his eyes.

"Danny!" Kay repeated. "Someone's at the door."

Finally, "Who's there?" he called.

"Open the door, Danny!" the thin voice said. "We've got to talk to you."

"It's the boys!" Kay said. "Now what?"

They slipped into their robes. Danny crossed to the door and unlocked it.

"Hey!" Matt said, pushing past his brother and Danny to get inside. "I thought we were never going to get you awake!"

"What are you guys doing up at this time of night?" Danny whispered. "You ought to be in bed and asleep."

Mark and Gil came into the cabin and closed the door behind them.

"D-D-Danny," Mark stammered, "you're not going to believe this, but we heard a flash in the water. I mean we saw a light flash in the water."

"And we heard something drop off the ship," Gil contributed. "Only it was a lifeboat and–"

"Now guys," Orlis said, "just simmer down and let's get this straight. Start at the beginning and let's hear from one at a time."

Gil started the story with Mark and Matt breaking in to fill in details until the account was finished.

"Now the lifeboat is gone!" Gil concluded. "I mean it's off the davits."

"Not very far," Matt put in. "We could see it floating out there!"

"Let's go topside," Danny said. "See what we can find out."

They started for the door. Kay moved beside Danny and took his hand.

"Are you going along?" he asked.

"You don't need to think you're going to leave me after a story like that," she said. "Not in the middle of the night."

They made their way silently to the top deck. The moon had come from behind the cloud and the scene was bathed in soft, mellow light.

"Boys!" Danny said, turning to them, "the lifeboat is there where it's always been!"

They just stared.

"This isn't another of your jokes, is it?" Orlis asked.

"We give you our word," Matt retorted. "It was out in the water when we saw it."

"Strange," Danny murmured.

He went to the lifeboat and examined it. In addition to serving as a lifeboat the *JUANITA MIA* used the small dinghy for certain kinds of fishing, so it was equipped with an outboard motor and a long anchor rope. Danny stood on the railing and reached over to feel the heavy line that held the anchor.

"You're right!" he exclaimed. "This boat has not only been in the water; it was anchored there!"

"But why?" Kay asked.

"Something I can't tell you," he replied.

"What are we going to do, Danny?" Mark asked.

"Right now," Danny said, "I think we'd all better go to bed. We'll talk this over in the morning after some sleep."

"Suits me," Mark agreed. "I sure don't hanker to meet the guy who was using that boat."

Danny nodded.

"Now you're talking sense," he said. "You'd better stay in your cabin until morning. You could get into real trouble prowling around."

"Don't worry about us," Matt said. "When we get to our cabin, I'm bolting the door. I'm staying there!"

They all quietly went below.

When Danny and Kay were gone the boys locked their door and checked it.

"Now, I'd like to see someone get in," Mark bragged.

"It looks to me as if we're going to have trouble getting out," his brother said. "But that suits me fine. I don't want to take chances on Brad Simmons coming in here!"

Gil Adrian sat down heavily on his bunk. He remained motionless, making no move to get back into bed for some time.

"Aren't you going to bed?" Mark asked.

"Wouldn't do any good," he said. "I couldn't sleep."

"I was just as scared," Matt said, "but I know I'll be able to sleep. I'm bushed."

"It's not that," Gil continued. "Being scared, I mean."

"What is it, then?" one of the twins asked.

"Those verses you read in the Bible," Gil Adrian began. "They don't mean what they sound like they mean, do they?"

"I'm not so sure I know what *you* mean," Mark said.

"A person doesn't have to become a Christian in order to go to heaven, does he?" Gil asked. "I mean if he lives a good life and does everything he's sup-posed to do, he'll get along okay, won't he? He'd go to heaven, wouldn't he?"

Matt and Mark both came wide awake.

"The Bible says we can't be good enough to earn our way into heaven," Matt answered. "It says that none of us is righteous, none of us seeks after God. It tells that we all sin."

"And," Mark put in, "it says *the wages of sin is death, but the gift of God is eternal life through Jesus Christ, our Lord.*"

Gil sat bent over. At last he looked up.

"I–I don't want to be lost." he said brokenly. "I do want to go to heaven."

"So do we," Matt said. "That's why we confessed our sin and accepted Jesus as our Savior."

"I–I don't even know how to pray," Gil managed.

"That's all right," Mark replied. "Praying is just talking to God. You know how to talk to people. If a person really means it, God will know and hear him."

They knelt beside Gil Adrian in their cabin.

* * *

Next morning when Danny and Kay went to the dining saloon, the twins and Gil came over to them.

"Hi, boys," Danny said, winking. "Did you guys have a good sleep?"

The boys smiled.

"Gil's got something to tell you, Danny," Matt said.

The tall, somber-faced boy moved closer.

"I–I just wanted to tell you," he stammered, "that I'm a Christian." He told them then what had happened.

Kay's eyes filled with tears.

"Oh, Gil!" she said softly so she wouldn't embarrass him. "I'm so happy for you."

"That's great," Danny said, shaking Gil's hand. "That's one decision you'll never regret."

"I feel a lot better already," Gil answered.

They were still talking when Dixie came hurrying to their table.

"Oh, Danny, Kay!" she said excitedly, "I've got to talk to you!"

She looked around and noted that others were staring.

Danny and Kay got up and followed her onto the deck. The boys tagged along plainly curious. Dixie was so disturbed she didn't notice them.

"What's the trouble?" Orlis asked.

"I found my camera!" she exclaimed. "Behind some old boxes in a storage closet."

"What would it be doing there?" Kay asked.

"That's what I don't know," Dixie said. "But I know this much. I didn't put it there."

"That's strange," Danny mused.

"That's not all!" she continued. "I went into my dark room just now! Someone had forced the door open and had developed some film or something. None of the equipment is the way I leave it."

"Wait!" Danny exclaimed. "That flash the boys saw in the water and that boat out there! Maybe this adds up."

He turned to talk to the twins and Gil. They were disappearing down the stairs!

Danny started after them.

"What are you going to do?" Kay called.

"Going to take a look at that dark room," he said. "I'm going to have a talk with the boys, go see Wilbur Adrian."

Before he could get to the improvised dark room Dixie had set up in a large closet at the end of the passageway, he saw Matt, Mark, and Gil Adrian steal cautiously out of it. Their faces lit up when they saw him.

"All right," he said, smiling. "What have you guys been up to?"

"Danny!" Mark exclaimed in a hoarse whisper, "we know who broke into this dark room. For sure! We've got the evidence to prove it!"

"All right, Sherlock Holmes," Orlis answered, "let's hear it!"

For answer Mark took a large white button from his pocket. He held it out to Danny.

"Who wears a suit coat with buttons like this?" he asked.

Danny turned it over in his hand.

"Only one man with a coat like this aboard the *JUANITA MIA*," he answered.

"Right!" Gil Adrian broke in. "I've known the guy all along. Brad Simmons!"

"Be careful!" Matt warned. "Don't talk so loud when you mention that guy's name! He'll clobber us if he finds out we're onto him."

Danny Orlis was thoughtful for a time.

"This fits together," he said. "It's beginning to make sense."

"What do you mean?" the boys asked curiously.

"Come along," Danny said. "You'll find out."

CHAPTER 11

MAN OVERBOARD
- NEAR DEATH

Danny and the three boys filed into Mr. Adrian's cabin.

"We'd like to talk with you for a few minutes, Wilbur," Danny began.

"You all look serious," Mr. Adrian replied, glancing from one to the other. "What seems to be troubling you?"

"We *are* serious, Dad," Gil told him. "There's something screwy going on."

Danny began at the beginning and told Mr. Adrian everything. Wilbur Adrian's eyes narrowed.

"That's the end!" he exclaimed hotly when Orlis finished. "I don't care what Krotter and Prescott say. I'm taking Brad ashore and leaving him at the village. I should never have let them talk me into bringing him in the first place. I was opposed right from the start."

He got to his feet and went storming out.

"Well," Matt observed, relief evident in his voice, "I guess that takes care of Brad Simmons."

"I hope so," Danny said evenly. "I sincerely hope so."

The boys wanted to go topside, but Danny thought it better to remain below.

"I'd just as soon Simmons gets off the *JUANITA MIA* before we go up," Danny said.

They waited until they thought surely Brad was gone. When they went up on deck, Captain D'Armando was just lowering a ladder to the stubby little powerboat. Brad Simmons and Wilbur Adrian were standing nearby, also a couple of swarthy crew members.

Brad turned to Danny.

"This is your doing!" he snarled.

"Is it?" Orlis asked.

"You know it is," Simmons repeated. "You and those brats! But I'll get you all if it's the last thing I do!"

"That's enough of that talk," Adrian said sternly. "We're ready to leave. Let's get on with it."

Brad turned defiantly before going down the rope ladder to the powerboat.

"Just remember what I told you!" he said ominously.

When they were gone Danny and the boys turned away from the railing.

"I'm sure glad he's gone," Gil said.

"So am I," Mark added. "There's only one thing. I wish we knew why he did the things he did. There had to be some reason."

Danny was thoughtful for a moment.

"You know, Mark," he said. "You've got a point. I was so anxious to get him out of here I didn't think about what he's been doing."

He looked up. Captain D'Armando was on the bridge.

"Let's go up and get the key to Brad's cabin," he said. "There may be a clue there. They hustled him off so fast he must have just had time enough to dump his things in a suitcase. He might not have had time to take everything. Especially if it was something hidden away."

The captain gave them the key and they went to the cabin Brad Simmons had used.

Mark said, "We can go through this cabin without worrying about Brad sneaking in on us."

They set to work. They removed dresser drawers, took cushions from the chair, and looked under the mattress, but there was no sign of anything left.

"He got out on the run," Gil said, "but it looks as though he cleaned up things pretty well. Maybe he figured something like this might happen and had his stuff where he could get it quickly."

"Could be," Danny said. "I suppose we might as well go. It doesn't look as though we're going to find anything."

Matt and Gil moved toward the door, but Mark remained where he was standing in the middle of the floor.

"Are you coming or not?" Matt demanded.

"I suppose this is silly," Mark said, "but there's one place where we didn't look. Behind that picture on the bulkhead."

"What could you hide behind a picture?" Matt asked scornfully.

Danny strode over and took the picture from its nail.

"Nope," he said. "Nothing here."

"What did I tell you?" Matt bragged.

Gil Adrian came up behind Danny Orlis and studied the picture.

"It looks to me as though the nail has been taken out and driven in again," Gil said.

Danny tried it with his fingers. "You're right!" he said. "It's loose! So is this one!"

In an instant Danny removed the brads from the picture frame and then the cardboard backing.

"Look!" Danny cried.

Behind the cardboard backing in the frame was another picture, one which none of them had ever seen!

"That was taken under the water, wasn't it?" Mark asked.

"And at night," Danny said. "This is the picture taken when you guys saw the flash last night."

"Do you really think so?" Matt asked.

Orlis nodded. "I'm positive," he said.

For two or three minutes they studied it. The picture was a closeup of a strange, cylindrical piece of coral. A steel tape line pulled out to 6 feet was fastened to it.

"What is it?" Matt asked. "Why would Brad be so anxious to have a picture of something like this? It certainly doesn't look like anything he'd want."

"But it is something," Danny answered. "Something very important."

He studied the picture some more.

"This is a picture of one of the guns on the man of war that's sunk on the reef below us," he said. "By taking measurements of the gun it is possible to determine just which wreck has been found. Records have been kept of the ships that have gone down for the past several hundred years, you know."

"I didn't know that," Mark said, "but I guess there are a lot of things I don't know."

"You can say that again," Matt muttered.

"Brad Simmons couldn't get the gun off the mounts and raise it," Danny continued, "and he wouldn't have dared, because of us, even if he could have done it. He did the next best thing. He stole Dixie's underwater camera, and took pictures of it with the tape measure as a means of comparison. With this picture it is possible for him to determine the size and bore of the gun, close enough, that is, to get a good clue as to the ship that's down there."

"I still don't see what good that will do him," Gil protested.

"That book Krotter took from Mr. Hale's," Danny said, "has the measurements of the ships and their armaments, if any, and a manifest, or list of the cargo she carried. It even has the last known location before they went down.”

“Then Brad could take that book and know whether the ship actually carried gold or not,” Matt put in.

“Right,” Danny answered. “It would tell where it was, how it was kept, and the form it is in.”

The boys were wide-eyed at once.

“This picture *is* important, then!” Gil observed. “Brad will be back for it! You can count on that!”

“Maybe,” Mark said, “and maybe not. There were two flashes, you know. He took at least two pictures and maybe more! He’s probably got the others with him!”

“Let’s go see about that book,” Danny suggested. “Maybe we’ve got something to thank Brad Simmons for. He could have saved us a lot of work.”

Danny got Dixie to go and see about the book. In a moment or two she was back.

“Lars looked all over for it,” she said, “but it’s gone!

Danny took a deep breath.

“Brad Simmons!” Matt said. “He’s the one who got it!”

“Go get Stan,” Orlis said suddenly. “He and I have got to dive before Simmons comes back!”

“Comes back?” Matt raised his voice. “Are you expecting him?”

“If he thinks there’s gold on this ship below us, he’ll be back.”

Danny hurried down to his cabin and changed into his swimming gear.

"I wish you weren't going to dive, Danny," Kay said.

"Don't worry, honey, I'm not going to take chances."

By the time he came on deck with his diving gear, Stan Wheeler was there staring into the cool, green water.

"All set?" Danny asked.

"I don't know," Stan replied uneasily. "Are those what I think they are?"

Danny Orlis stared too.

There were two large dorsal fins slicing through the water. As he looked, another and still another surfaced.

"Sharks!"

Stan swallowed hard.

"You aren't planning on diving, are you?" he asked.

"Not today," Danny assured him. "There isn't enough money down there to make me go after it with those fellows in the territory."

They went to the railing and watched the sharks with irresistible fascination.

Time passed swiftly.

After an hour or so Danny said, "I think I'll go below and change."

"Good idea," Stan added, "and while I'm at it, I think I'll go below and get some shut-eye."

With a last look at the sharks Stan disappeared down the stairs.

"I'd like to know why those sharks appeared all of a sudden," Orlis observed thoughtfully. "It doesn't seem logical."

"They sure ruined things when it came to keeping you and Stan from diving," Gil said.

Danny went below and changed to other clothes.

"I'm glad you didn't dive," Kay told him. "I've been terribly concerned about you all day. In fact, I just finished praying for you."

"Thank you, my dear," he said. "It always makes me feel good to know that you are praying for me."

He sat down on the bunk and had just reached for his sock when Matt came blasting into their cabin.

"Danny!" he cried breathlessly. "Come quick!"

"What's the matter?" Danny demanded, leaping to his feet.

"There's a motorboat with one man coming this way!" Matt gasped.

Orlis started for the stairs on the run.

"You'd better stay here, Kay," he called over his shoulder. "I'll be sending the boys for you to look after."

By the time Danny and Matt reached the deck the boat was nudging the *JUANITA MIA*.

"Brad Simmons!" Danny called. "What are you doing back here?"

"Come back to pay you a little visit, Gov'nor," he said. "I got a score to settle!"

He climbed over the railing. Danny took a hurried look about; the boys had melted away out of sight. He was thankful for that.

"I thought maybe you'd go diving with my little playmates, Gov'nor," Brad continued, grinning. "You didn't know old Brad was smart enough to bait 'em in to keep you from divin', did you? A little bloody meat! That's all it takes in these parts. Sharks are a heap better'n watch dogs."

Danny stood balancing lightly on the balls of his feet. Captain D'Armando! Why didn't the boys go and get *him* or one of the crew? He realized then that they were in a place where they could not get out without being seen.

"Your pals on shore are sure goin' to be s'prised when they find out I stole their boat," he said. "I've come back to get my picture and even things up with you."

All the while he kept inching forward, menacingly, one hand held slightly behind his back.

"I'm going to get you, Orlis!"

With that he drew the belaying pin from behind him.

"You're going to–"

He didn't get to finish what he was saying!

The Maxwell twins and Gil Adrian came charging out of their hiding place, fanned out, then went bearing down on Simmons like tacklers rushing a kicker.

"Get him, Danny!" Mark cried. "Help us get him!"

With a snarl of rage Brad Simmons tensed, raising the heavy belaying pin above his head.

Danny sprang at him, his shoulder and head down in blocking position, one hand reaching for Brad's upraised arm. He hit the surprised Simmons in the chest and sent him hurtling backward. Brad smashed into the rail. It broke under the impact, and he tumbled into the water. Danny almost plunged in after him.

There was a thud as Brad squarely hit the little boat below them. For a brief instant he teetered on the little deck, then toppled into the shark-infested water.

All that took place quickly, in a matter of a second or two. Those on the *JUANITA MIA*, who heard the commotion, couldn't reach the spot fast enough to witness it.

Danny caught himself and hung on momentarily, shaking his head. For an instant everything spun around him. Then things began to clear, and he straightened to stare down into the water.

Brad was floating motionless some five or ten feet away from the little boat. His fall had not gone unobserved. The sharks, who had been fed from the deck of the *JUANITA MIA*, were moving expectantly toward him.

"Go down into that boat!" Danny shouted to the boys. "Be ready to help us aboard!"

With that Danny dove into the water!

His dive was clean and true. He sliced into the gently rolling waves just a scant yard from Brad Simmons. Grasping the injured man by the hair he swam hurriedly to the small boat.

A small shark raced toward them, wicked jaws agape.

Matt lashed out with an oar, hitting the fish with a glancing blow on the side of the head. It was enough to deflect his aim and it caused him to miss Danny and Brad by just inches.

Another stroke and Danny brought Brad to the boat. The boys helped get the unconscious man into it. Danny scrambled in himself. By the time he got clear of the water, at least half a dozen sharks were pressing in about the area.

CHAPTER 12

WHOSOEVER COMES IS NEVER CAST OUT

The next day Danny Orlis went down to the cabin where they had taken the injured Brad Simmons. The *JUANITA MIA* was under full power, plowing toward the mainland and a doctor.

"How is he?" Danny asked.

Brad rolled over and groaned weakly.

Kay nodded. "He seems to be conscious most of the time," she answered.

"I want to talk to you, Gov'nor," Simmons managed to say, his voice thin and weak.

"Is it all right, Kay?" Danny asked his wife.

"I think so. If you don't talk too long."

"Where they takin' me?" Brad asked.

"To a doctor," Danny said. "You picked up a nasty head bump when you fell into that powerboat."

Brad nodded. For several more minutes he did not speak.

"They say you fished me out," Brad said at last. "Risked your neck doing it."

Danny made no reply.

"Why'd you do it, Gov'nor?" Brad asked. "I wouldn't have done it for you."

"Because I'm a Christian," Danny said simply.

The peculiar look came back to Brad's face once more.

"Know what I'm going to do?" Brad continued. "Soon as I get over this, I'm going to take you guys back to the reef and help get the treasure out of that ship if someone else hasn't found it. There's supposed to be a fortune there. You can cut me in or not. Just as you like."

"I'm sure the men will appreciate that, Brad," Danny told him. "I'm happy that you want to do it. I'm going to be much too busy to go along again."

"You mean you'd turn down a chance to get your share?" the wounded man asked weakly.

"I'm going to be working on something more precious than gold," Danny said. "I'm going to be bringing the gospel to the lost."

He watched Brad closely.

"May I ask you a question?" Orlis said suddenly.

The man on the bed nodded.

"Every time I've mentioned things of Christ to you, you've bristled. Are you running away from God, Brad?"

Simmon's body stiffened and his eyes glistened.

"You've heard the way of salvation many times, haven't you?" Danny persisted.

"From my mother's knee," Brad said weakly, "but I wasn't going to give in to anything like that!"

"Don't you want to confess your sin now and accept Christ *now?*" Danny asked him gently.

Brad's voice choked.

"Do–do you think God would have me?" he asked.

"*Whosoever comes unto me,*" Danny quoted, "*I will in no wise cast out.*"

Danny and Kay Orlis knelt beside the bunk. As Brad Simmons made a real but weak attempt to pray, the Maxwell twins, Matt and Mark, with Gil Adrian came in quietly. They all knelt beside Danny and Kay. Soon Kay suggested that they leave so that Brad could rest.

THE DANNY ORLIS SERIES

The Danny Orlis series, by Bernard Palmer, delivers a blend of adventure, mystery, and suspense through various settings—from the Canadian wilderness to Guatemalan jungles. Danny Orlis, an adept outdoorsman, skilled athlete, and committed Christian, employs his quick thinking, calm bravery, and biblical solutions to confront everyday problems and hair-raising dangers. Early stories focus on Danny navigating school life, sports, and outdoor challenges, while in later books, Danny and his wife Kay provide wisdom and guidance to youngsters facing lifelike situations and challenges. Having sold over two million copies, this series has made Palmer a renowned author in Christian youth literature. Palmer is also the author of the Felicia Cartright series and various other series for Christian youth.

AVAILABLE FROM WWW.ANEKOPRESS.COM